Two Secret Sins

A Scandal in Mayfair Book 2

ANNA CAMPBELL

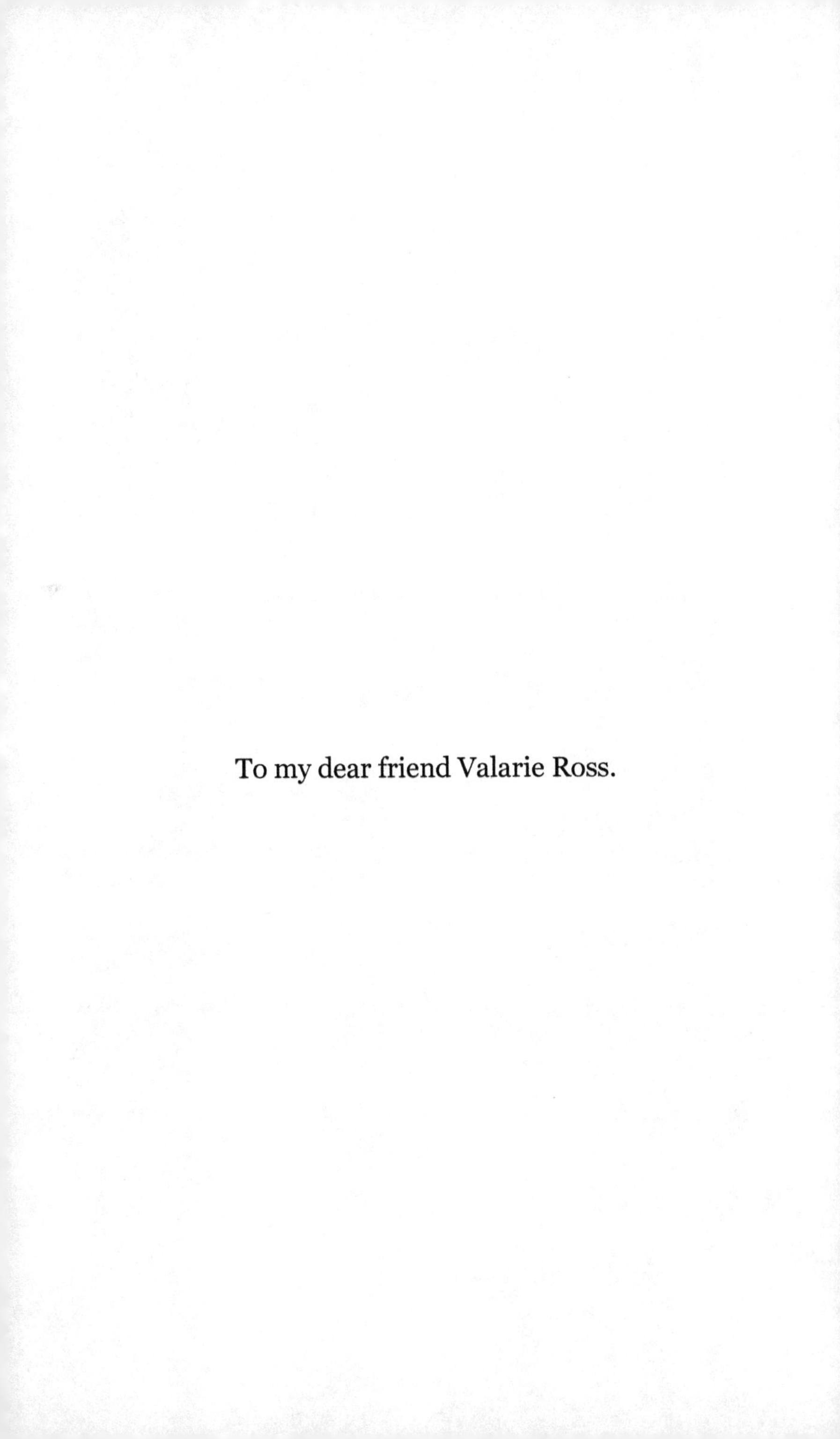

To my dear friend Valarie Ross.

CHAPTER ONE

Half Moon Street, Mayfair, London, March 1816

Eliot Ridley, Viscount Colville, stepped back to survey the perfect globes of his mistress's bare buttocks, presented to him as she bent over the carved base of her bed. By heaven, he was the luckiest fellow in England.

His hands caught Verena's luscious rump, as he leaned in to kiss that firm white flesh. This close to her sex, the rich scent of her excitement invaded his senses. He breathed deep, loving that she wanted him just as much as he wanted her.

Under his mouth, she shifted in encouragement. "Don't wait, Eliot," she said in a constricted voice. With her stomach crushed against the wooden edge, catching enough breath to speak must be difficult. She quivered in response as he nipped her.

"Spread your legs wider," he said gruffly, too on edge for niceties as he rose behind her.

She obeyed, sliding her feet further apart across the carpet, and hitched upward until he could see her sleek pink cleft. He repositioned his grip on her hips and thrust forward with a smoothness that took him to the hilt. As his body sank into hers, his soul sank into immediate peace. Which seemed mad, when he was as sexually aroused as a man could be. But since their first encounter, Verena had always had this magical effect on him.

As he basked in her hot, wet clasp, he sucked in a huge breath. It felt like his first full breath in a month.

Sighing with pleasure, she clenched around him as if she never meant to let him go. For a long moment, they remained still, captive to the mighty power of this connection. Then, with an incoherent grumble deep in her throat, she bumped back. He took the hint and began to move in long, hard, possessive strokes that penetrated to the place inside her that drove her wild.

"Oh, yes," she gasped, as she began to shake. "More."

Eliot smiled with tigerish intent and released her hips to catch her waist. While she shuddered and writhed through a storm of feminine pleasure, he kept moving.

He bent over her to caress the full breasts that bobbed with every thrust. Her whimper of surrender became another melting sigh. She reached back to give his face a clumsy caress, then her hand dropped down to fist in the sheets as another wave hit her hard.

Eliot's balls were aching and, despite his best intentions, his thrusts became less measured. In a perfect world, he'd maintain this relentless rhythm that she loved until she called a halt, but in this one, he was too close to climax to last much longer.

She must have felt it because with a brief grunt of amusement, she nudged back once more. "Will you let me finish you?" she murmured, her voice husky after her lengthy orgasm.

As he pulled free, he couldn't summon any words. Dear Lord, he could barely summon a coherent thought. He straightened and stepped away on unsteady legs.

She braced her arms against the base of the bed and rose. He couldn't doubt that he'd satisfied her. Her uncharacteristic awkwardness told him that pleasure still rippled through her. "On the bed or here?"

"Here," he said and almost lost himself as she fell to her knees before him.

Verena's hungry gaze settled on the erect penis jutting toward her. Her greedy anticipation thundered through him like a herd of runaway horses. He shuddered again when she cradled his balls, then encircled that column of swollen flesh with her hand.

"Don't...don't be too long about it," he managed to croak out, which drew another huff of amusement from her.

The amusement faded, and her expression became intent. Her hold firmed as with the ease and eagerness that always made his heart perform acrobatics, she took him into her mouth.

More heat. More pressure. More blazing pleasure. Her lips began to move on him, and he buried his unsteady hand in her tumble of mahogany hair as he yielded to the invincible rise to completion.

On a muffled growl, she increased the pressure. That ruined any chance of holding back. Verena knew a thousand ways of teasing him until he was half-mad. But today, he was too close to the brink to extend their play.

He angled forward and on a guttural groan, he delivered himself up to her. Digging his fingers into her skull, he jerked helplessly into her mouth. She took every drop with an avidity that only intensified his ecstasy.

At last, he managed to step away on legs that were near to collapse. She sat back on her heels and raised one hand to wipe her lips. Her blue eyes were dark, and alive with sensual knowledge. And wicked self-satisfaction with what she'd just done. Verena liked knowing that he couldn't resist her.

Shaking, he retreated until his hand met the bedpost. He needed its help to stay standing.

As she took in his wobbly state, Verena smiled. "I can see you missed me."

Missed her? This last month on the family estate had lasted an eon. He'd tried to leave Hamble Park after a fortnight, but his business dealings had been more complicated than expected and his oaf of a father had been as intransigent as usual. In good conscience, he hadn't been able to escape back to London until now.

At a furious clip, he'd driven to Lorimer Square where he left his carriage in his father's stables. Then instead of calling into his rooms at the Albany, he'd headed straight to Verena's elegant house. The lack of her these last weeks had left him restless and unhappy and out of sorts.

He told her none of that. Instead, his lips curled in wry acknowledgement. "A little."

Her smile deepened. "You needed that."

"I did."

Turning up today, he'd broken a longstanding arrangement. It was Wednesday, while until now, he always visited on Friday afternoons. When he'd let himself into the garden and knocked on the French doors, he hadn't been sure whether Verena would give him his marching orders or invite him into her bed.

Her hatchet-faced butler Merton had shown him into the gold and white drawing room. When Verena joined him, Eliot had prepared for some complaint about his extended absence. But she'd taken one glance at his face, and whatever she'd seen there had her rushing over to fling her arms around him and deliver a passionate, open-mouthed kiss.

Within minutes, his breeches gaped open, and he was heaving and grunting over her as she sprawled across the priceless Turkey carpet. Their first fuck downstairs had been hot and fierce and over within minutes. After he'd caught his breath and fastened his breeches, she took him by the hand and led him up to her bedroom.

He felt like he hadn't done her justice in the drawing room, although she'd reached her peak with a little help from his hand on her quim. The incendiary memory rushed through him and despite his exhaustion, he felt a distant spark of interest.

She always melted into climax with a naturalness that thrilled him. He'd never known a woman so frank about how she relished the sexual act. There was nothing shy about Verena Gerard. Right from the first, she'd demonstrated no trace of shame or shock at anything that they did together. Her attitude to sex was like a man's. Even more practical than most of the men he knew. When she wanted something, she set out to get it.

Right now and for the last six months, she'd wanted Eliot Ridley. When their affair started, her enthusiasm and daring had been a glorious surprise. Her appetite for pleasure and her refusal to apologize for her powerful urges still enthralled him.

Verena rose to her feet and wandered across to the door of the dressing room. He studied the perfect line of her back and the gentle movement of those round buttocks. She was a creature of delicious curves, perfectly shaped to fit his hands.

She turned in the doorway, giving him the chance to feast on the sight of the pointed pink nipples that he loved to kiss. His gaze traced the pale plain of her stomach and the nest of dark brown curls at the juncture of her thighs. That niggle of interest became a little more urgent, although he was nowhere near ready for another bout.

Verena was a beautiful woman, and most beautiful of all when she was naked. Partly because she didn't display an ounce of self-consciousness. She had a body created for pleasure, and she knew it.

"I missed you, too," she said in a careless way, as if it didn't mean anything.

Verena might be incapable of shock, but Eliot still was.

As she disappeared into the dressing room, astonishment crashed through him, stole his breath. He couldn't believe his ears. Theirs was a relationship built purely on physical compatibility. They didn't swap confidences or whisper sweet endearments to each other in the cuddly aftermath to sex.

They didn't partake of many cuddly aftermaths. Most of the time, Verena sent him on his way, once he'd satisfied her urges. She didn't share her troubles with him. Nor did her sympathetic hand on his brow soothe away the difficulties of his day.

Although on numerous occasions, she'd offered him relief from his worries and annoyances with a good fuck. He had no complaints about that.

Lady Verena Gerard didn't stay with her lovers for long, although while she did, she was faithful. Her affair with Eliot constituted one of her more enduring liaisons. Which meant that while he'd arrived here today frantic to have her, he hadn't been sure if after a month's absence, he still counted as her lover.

Given what they'd done this afternoon, he guessed that he still did.

By the time that she returned to the bed, smelling of jasmine soap and wrapped in a ruby velvet peignoir that complemented her pink and white complexion, he'd convinced himself not to make too much of what she'd said.

After giving her a swift kiss, he went through to clean himself up. Verena's well-trained and discreet servants always made sure that hot water and refreshments were set out in the dressing room. He'd turned up in all his travel dirt, but he'd been in such a lather to see his mistress that he'd been unable to wait. He was shamingly aware that a gentleman should have taken the trouble to wash and shave before he called on a lady.

Eliot pulled on his breeches and poured two brandies, before he stepped back into the shadowy bedroom. Verena was ranged on the bed, lolling against the pile of pillows. The loose peignoir sagged open over her generous bosom. With her kiss-swollen lips and cascade of dark hair, she looked thoroughly debauched.

He smiled in masculine appreciation and leaned one shoulder against the doorjamb. "I've brought you a brandy."

"Thank you," she said, holding out her hand as he straightened and approached. He delivered the drink and bent to brush a kiss across her ruffled hair.

He crossed to stand at the window, watching the late afternoon light fade across her garden. Spring was tardy arriving this year. The spindly trees held a hint of green, but the daffodils were yet to appear. Traffic noise seeped in from the street in front of the house, but right now, he felt like he and Verena shared a private bubble. It was a deuced pleasant fantasy.

He sipped his drink and let his mind dwell on what they'd just done. What they might do next.

"Are you at leisure this evening?" He turned to face her. "I could stay."

What Eliot really wanted was a night alone with Verena. The last few weeks had been hell, yet the sight of his headstrong mistress made all the vexations go away. He wasn't ready to step out of this opulent bedroom and face the world's clamor once again.

With a shake of her lovely head, she set her half-empty glass on the nightstand. "I'm engaged for dinner at Celia Edgecombe's."

Verena didn't sound particularly disappointed to send Eliot on his way. Why would she? She enjoyed his company. She enjoyed having his cock inside her even more. But neither were essential to her well-being, whereas he thought of her all the time and his desire for her verged on obsession.

It was damnable being at her mercy, but he couldn't break free. Theirs was a deuced strange affair.

She was such a goddess in his arms, that it was a risk trying to change things between them. Yet he couldn't help taking that risk.

He finished his brandy and set the glass down on top of the chest of drawers. "Would you like to go driving tomorrow?"

His invitation made her raise her eyebrows in surprise. "In Hyde Park?"

"If you like."

She gave a gurgle of laughter. "You're in a bizarre humor today, my lord. Time with your family always puts you on edge."

He frowned and swung away to the window again. "Time with my father does. Imogen and Stella are perfectly acceptable company." In a week, his younger sister Imogen arrived in London for her first season. Stella, his cousin, acted as Imogen's companion and chaperone. "So will you come out in my carriage?"

As he posed the question, he knew what her answer would be.

"I won't."

No, she wouldn't. In the half a year that they'd been together, they'd managed to keep their liaison a secret from the nosiest society on earth. It was something of a miracle. The fact that they made such an unlikely couple helped preserve their privacy. Nobody would imagine Lord Colville and Lady Verena Gerard feeling anything for each other except polite disdain.

But the moment that Eliot caught a glimpse of the notorious widow at a hunt meet in Leicestershire, he'd known she was the one for him. He'd been staying with a friend in the neighborhood. It turned out that Verena, who was a punishing rider, had a hunting box nearby.

He'd heard of her, of course. A woman so beautiful and so profligate with her favors couldn't help sparking gossip. If anyone had asked him, although nobody was likely to, he'd have said that such an undiscriminating female wasn't to his taste.

So he'd been unprepared for the impact of that luscious brunette beauty and that wild, joyous spirit. In an instant, all his starchy judgements had crumbled to dust.

Because Verena wasn't cheap and shabby and desperate. She was the most vivid person he'd ever met, and in her company, for the first time in his well-behaved existence, he felt alive. As if he emerged from a long dark tunnel into radiant light.

If his friends ever found out about the affair, they'd be astonished that he'd fallen under this particular lady's spell. Yet Eliot wasn't surprised at all. Verena's warmth and thirst for experience were irresistible to a man who had spent his entire life in the cold. Her presence offered perpetual summer, whereas winter touched everything else around him.

It was no extraordinary thing that Eliot should want Verena Gerard. What was extraordinary was that Verena returned his interest.

Eliot was counted a virtuous, upright member of society, a model of decorum, a man who never set a foot wrong, destined for great things. His ambitious father, Lord Deerforth, had groomed his only son since childhood for political power.

A liaison between a future prime minister and the brazen widow was unthinkable.

When they met, Eliot feared Verena would dismiss him as a dull dog. A fellow too wrapped up in his own rectitude to attract her. The previous men who shared her bed had all been dashing rakes. While Eliot had always been more complicated than his correct manners might indicate, not even in his wildest dreams would he describe himself as either dashing or a rake.

But when their eyes met over the baying of hounds and the buzz of conversation, some silent message had passed between them. Two days later, he'd called at her house on his way back to Gloucestershire, and she'd taken him into her bed. For three days, he'd dwelled in a heaven that surpassed all previous experience. And despite the virtuous façade that he presented to the world, he was a man who had known his fair share of women.

From the first, he and Verena had both recognized that it was better that nobody knew they were together. But as time went on with no lessening in his interest, he grew impatient with the small part that she allowed him to play in her life.

Now, when she refused him, he didn't turn to look at her. "I'm not ashamed of you, you know."

A bristling silence greeted that. He realized with a sinking heart how patronizing he sounded. Before he could muster an apology, she responded with a hint of acid. "Well, that's gratifying to hear. Perhaps instead, I'm ashamed of you."

Aghast, he turned to face her. "Damn it, Verena, you don't mean that."

The eyes that she leveled on him were cool. How could she turn his blood to steam with her touch, yet look at him as if he was little more than an acquaintance? An annoying acquaintance, at that. "Don't I?"

He bit back the urge to beg her forgiveness. She already had too much advantage over him. "Perhaps it's time I left."

Even as he spoke, he knew that she wouldn't fall for his games. She stayed where she was and took a sip of her brandy. "Perhaps you should. I need to deal with a few things before I go out tonight."

Eliot bowed, while some horrified corner of his mind panicked at the idea that one of those "things" might be choosing a new lover. After all, they'd never made any promises to each other. He should appreciate a mistress who made no demands beyond physical pleasure. Instead the uncertainty sent him completely demented.

He was free to move on when he wanted to, as was she. And he hated it.

"I bid you good afternoon, then," he said stiffly, knowing that he was behaving like an idiot, but unable to stop himself. The glint of mocking humor in Verena's dark blue eyes didn't make him feel any better.

Her calmness remained unruffled. "Goodbye, Eliot."

Goodbye? Surely not. "What about Friday?"

And every day after that?

She arched her eyebrows. "I believe we have an appointment." She paused, and he waited in an agony of suspense for her to break with him. "Unless you'd rather make other arrangements."

Other arrangements? By God, yes, he would. He'd like to bundle her up and carry her away to a place where he could slake his passions on her for months on end. He'd like to see Verena, without worrying about a thousand curious eyes watching on. He'd like to have her to himself. He'd like to know that he wasn't alone in finding the strength of this attraction completely disorienting.

None of that was possible. Although at least she wasn't sending him away forever.

"I don't want to make other arrangements." His voice was flat, as he struggled to hide the powerful relief that flooded him. One day, they would be done, but that day wasn't today.

The straight look that Verena gave him sent a chill sliding down his spine. "Nor do I."

It was a message that he was smart enough to understand. *Don't take this affair out into the public domain. Don't ask for more than I want to give you. Don't attempt to make a perfectly satisfying carnal connection into anything more profound.*

"Excellent." When he bowed again, it was as much to acknowledge her command as to take his leave. "I'll call on Friday."

Except that as he strolled through the darkening streets to his rooms on Piccadilly, the outcome didn't feel excellent. It felt as if Verena had slammed a door in his face. As she had.

He could have what they had now. Not a scrap more. Ever. Or he could walk away.

Walking away wasn't an acceptable alternative.

Over and over, Eliot had sinned with Verena. He hoped to sin with her again. Often.

But he'd committed one secret sin against her, a sin that would end their affair forever if she guessed the truth. In this sophisticated world they inhabited, falling in love wasn't an option.

Yet Eliot loved Verena Gerard so much, he was sick with it.

CHAPTER TWO

Verena didn't have to wait until Friday to see Eliot again, following that odd, troubling afternoon when he called on her without notice.

They didn't often attend the same parties, which was one of the reasons that it had taken them so long to meet. Viscount Colville was careful to keep his reputation pristine, and he moved in much more respectable circles than she did. He was a regular at Almack's and appeared at most of the debutante balls, whereas she was more likely to be flirting and waltzing at a naughty masquerade.

However much people might gossip about her, very few members of the beau monde shunned Verena for her outrageous behavior. Her father was the Duke of Horsham, and she was rich, and famed for her wit and elegance. In society's eyes, that made up for a lot of the tattle – most of which was true, she admitted without a shred of shame. And while she'd taken a string of lovers since her worm of a husband's unlamented death seven years ago, all of them had been highborn leaders of society.

An aristocratic widow was allowed a degree of freedom that neither an innocent young miss nor a wife enjoyed. As long as she wasn't falling pregnant with a footman's bastard or making scenes in public like poor, hysterical Caro Lamb, she remained acceptable to the ton.

When Verena joined the line of dancers at Lady Paget's ball on Thursday night, she cast a casual glance down the ranks and saw Eliot's gilt blonde hair gleaming in the candlelight. That color was unmistakable, unique. He was a good deal taller than most of the other men in the room, so she wondered how she'd missed his arrival. Something in the air always changed when Eliot walked into a room, but not this time.

Before she could remind herself that she was a jaded lady of thirty, her foolish heart skipped a beat. He was so handsome, like a hero from a fairy tale. Sir Galahad must have been just such a gilded paragon. Eliot Ridley's face was formed of pure sculpted planes, and his body was long and lean and covered from head to toe in smooth golden skin. As she knew very well.

In her imagination, she always pictured him wearing glittering armor. From the first moment she'd seen him, she'd sensed that he belonged to an earlier, more chivalrous age. Before they met, she'd even derided him to her friends as a boring prig, old before his time and starchy as a Bow Street judge.

She still saw him as unsuited to this modern world, with all its pettiness and compromises and meanness. After six months as his lover, she'd come to recognize his nobility of spirit.

Tonight Eliot wasn't wearing armor: it wouldn't do in a ballroom. Instead, he looked spectacular in severe black evening dress with a snowy white neckcloth that set off that sharply cut jaw.

"Verena?" Lord Shelburn, her partner for this dance, said to attract her attention.

With a start, she realized that she was staring at Eliot and her silly heart was still capering around like a spring lamb let loose in a sunny field. How could she be so careless? Goodness knew what her face might reveal.

It never ceased to amaze her that she and Eliot had managed to keep their affair secret. She was sure that someone must notice the way the air between them sizzled. But the idea of the wanton widow and the perfect Lord Colville being on fire for each other was just too outlandish to occur to the wider world.

While it required an effort, she adopted her usual cynical expression. In case she was blushing, she waved her fan in front of her face. When blushing, along with a susceptible heart, was something that she'd given up, back when she was a brainless ingenue.

"La, it's such a crush in here. I vow that we'd be more comfortable running around naked."

Shelburn's laugh held an appreciative note. "Please don't let me stop you from setting the fashion."

She cast him an arch glance, although the necessity for the old, stale games filled her with ennui. Verena had played this scene so often, that it was hard to summon much interest in her role as the coquette. "You first."

He laughed again and took her hand to start the promenade. Shelburn was an acknowledged rake and just the sort of flashy devil who she liked to invite into her bed. They'd never been lovers, although the possibility had always hovered.

Perhaps they would link up at last, once she and Eliot parted. Shelburn was wildly attractive, and she'd heard talk that he knew what to do with a woman. She wished to heaven that the prospect of finding out the truth about those rumors awakened the tiniest glimmer of interest.

As Verena paced forward, she turned her back on Eliot. She only identified his partner when she promenaded back to where she started. He was dancing with some pretty young thing. It took Verena a moment to remember the chit's name. Lily Bilson, one of the more successful debutantes this year. The sort of girl who would make Viscount Colville a perfect bride. Verena recovered from a stumble, as she joined hands with Shelburn and Freddie Edgecombe on her other side and circled around.

"Colville must be on the hunt for a wife," Shelburn said, his voice snide. "He could do worse than the Bilson filly. She has a large fortune, and she's a peach besides. Too good for that pompous ass, in fact. Any woman who marries Eliot Ridley is condemned to die of boredom."

Verena struggled against leaping to Eliot's defense. After all, she herself had said similar things about him in the past.

Before they met, she'd been convinced that Viscount Colville would despise any woman who was too free with her favors. But that was before she'd seen the burning hunger in his eyes and decided to satisfy her curiosity about how it would feel to seduce a saint. Her experiment had bitten back at her. She'd discovered that more than a little of the devil lurked beneath that pure exterior.

"It might be the viscount who dies of boredom," she said in a tone that she hoped indicated disinterest. "The girl looks like she hasn't got the brains God gave a sheep."

"A very decorative sheep." The hint of admiration in Shelburn's tone made Verena's skin itch.

Although, damn it, he was right. And the Bilson girl was twelve years younger than Verena, and a virgin besides. Definitely a suitable bride for Lord Colville. If she survived Verena's wrath long enough to accept any proposal that he made. Right now, Verena would be happy to rip every golden hair from that empty head. Anything to wipe away the chit's smile, as she stared at the handsome viscount in wonder.

Stay away from him. He's mine.

At least for now. Because the sad truth was that one day, sooner rather than later, he'd wed a sweet little poppet like Miss Bilson and have a string of lovely babies. He was accounted one of London's most eligible bachelors. Wealthy, wellborn, presentable, untarred with tawdry scandal. As beautiful as an angel. Heir to his father's title, and in line to become richer still when he inherited. Even if he was the dull dog that reputation painted him, he'd be credited as a catch.

"You're looking rather fierce." Shelburn's curiosity again reminded Verena of where she was and who she was with. "There's no need to feel you have to rescue the chit. I'm sure she can imagine no fate more appealing than popping out a brood of tedious little Ridleys."

To her relief, the dance shifted Verena onto her next partner, and she was saved from mustering a reply.

Inevitably as the line progressed, she found herself facing Eliot. The cool distance in his bow contradicted the heat flaring in his gaze. He caught her hand, and more heat rushed up under her skin.

Even through two pairs of gloves, that contact was searing.

As they began the promenade, he bent his head toward her and spoke in a low voice. "I'm sorry I was such a fool on Wednesday. Have you forgiven me?"

There were many things that she liked about Eliot, when she'd expected not to like him at all. Among them was that, unlike most men of her acquaintance, he was willing to admit if he was at fault.

She dared a quick glance at him from under her lashes. Anyone watching would think she flirted, as she was wont to do. But her look held more concern than coquetry. He sounded troubled, although his expression remained neutral. After six months, they had the masquerade down pat.

"Yes, I forgive you," she replied in an equally low voice.

She read his relief, and the hand holding hers tightened. "I shouldn't have come around that afternoon. But damn it, Verena, after putting up with my idiot of a father for a month, I needed to see you."

"I didn't mind." She hadn't lied about missing him, although in his absence, she'd done her best to divert herself with her friends and a constant round of balls and parties. Never let it be said that Lady Verena Gerard was so jejune as to pine for a man.

"You should have. Any gentleman would have gone home and made himself presentable, then sent a note around to ask if it was convenient to call."

A huff of wry laughter escaped her, as they turned to promenade back. "Then I'd have missed out on a memorable encounter. It brightened up an afternoon when I was at a loose end."

And restless and unhappy, because she wanted to see Eliot. When he turned up without warning and took her in a conflagration of passion on the floor, she'd almost swooned with sheer excitement. His urgent need had thrilled her to the toes.

She'd long ago discovered that he was a man of powerful urges and a lover of breathtaking finesse. But after he returned from the country, he'd been so mad for her. When she recalled the frantic edge of his possession, she still got goose bumps.

"You're too good to me."

Before she could refute that statement, they broke apart to form a circle. Their brief privacy was over. She moved down the line once more, knowing that her short conversation with Eliot promised to be the highlight of the evening. Even though she'd flirt and laugh and dance until well after midnight.

At first, pretending that Lord Colville was nothing to her had given her a secret frisson. Public strangers, private lovers. It was a game that she hadn't played before. But the need to be on her guard all the time was losing its charm. She suspected that it did for him, too.

For one fleeting instant on Wednesday, she'd wondered if she could accept his invitation to the park. But an association with Verena Gerard would only mire him in scandal and bring his political ambitions crashing down around him.

When she returned to Shelburn at the end of the dance, she was smiling and ironic as ever, but her heart wasn't at ease. Perhaps the time approached to move on from Eliot. Six months was a long time to be faithful to one man.

Now she saw a few disturbing signs that the viscount wished to change their arrangement. Worse, she started to rely on him for her happiness and well-being.

That wasn't permitted.

Verena pretended to pay attention to Celia Edgecombe, who was relating the latest *on dit*, while she tested the idea of sending Eliot away. It felt like pressing her tongue up against a sore tooth. If the idea of letting him go caused her distress, it was indeed time to move on. When her husband died, she'd sworn that no man would ever hurt her again, and for seven years, she'd kept that vow.

The thought of breaking with Eliot made everything in her rise up in protest. Never to feel the touch of his hands? Never to kiss him? Never again to enjoy that impressive masculine tackle? Tackle that would have been wasted on the puritan she'd once called him.

With the end of this affair, she'd miss more than a competent lover in her bed. With the end of this affair, she'd miss the rumble of a deep voice and a smile that lit silvery eyes, while not quite reaching his lips. Even more lowering to admit, she'd also miss the decency that invested every cell of Eliot's body.

Decency was a trait that she and her sophisticated friends often mocked. Something too dreary for such daring creatures as Verena and her crowd to espouse.

Decency had always sounded like such a banal quality. Perhaps because until she met Eliot, Verena hadn't seen much of it. Now she'd learned to value the goodness in him as much – well, almost – as she valued what he could do to her with that gorgeous body.

It was pleasant to be with a man who respected one's opinions, who didn't take one for granted, who didn't always expect his needs to be paramount. It was pleasant to be able to rely on Eliot's bone-deep kindness. Because at heart, he was a kind man. If Verena had witnessed little decency in her life, she'd seen even less kindness.

She'd once ridiculed Lord Colville as a saint. While perhaps he wasn't quite that, Eliot Ridley was the best man she'd ever known. Without question, Verena Gerard was bad for him. She wasn't worthy of him, and if word of their affair got out, she'd damage him, perhaps irreparably.

Yes, it was time to find another lover.

Yet as her eyes drifted with manufactured disinterest over to where he stood on the other side of the crowded room, laughing at something Lady Lumsden said, her heart ached at the idea. Another sign that she was overdue for a fresh adventure.

Verena's heart was locked away tight in a steel box. She'd long ago thrown away the key. If Eliot Ridley made that useless organ stir to life, the affair was becoming dangerous and she must end it.

No, no, no, said the heart that she refused to acknowledge.

CHAPTER THREE

*P*anting, exhausted, naked, Verena stretched out on the bed that she'd once shared with her brute of a husband. When Lord George Gerard, the second son of the Marquess of Trask, broke his neck in a hunting accident seven years ago, God had answered a maiden's prayer. Although by that stage, it was years since a violent wedding night had deprived her of her maidenhead.

After George's death, she'd completely redecorated her pretty little house in Half Moon Street. Now it reflected a refined feminine taste that her late husband would have detested. The bed was the only piece of furniture that she'd kept from those miserable six years of marriage.

On the night of George Gerard's funeral, she'd invited her first paramour to join her in this bed. Most of her joy in the act had come from knowing that George turned in his grave. If he didn't already burn in hell.

All her lovers since had shared her marital bed. Every time that she spasmed into ecstasy in a man's arms, she said a silent "To the devil with you,

George," to the selfish blackguard who had wed seventeen-year-old Lady Verena Charteris.

Or at least she had, until Eliot Ridley became her lover. It was another warning of unwelcome intimacy that when Eliot sent her up in flames, she didn't think about anyone but him.

A week had passed since Lady Paget's ball and Verena's decision to send her current lover on his way. As her current lover lay only several inches away after an energetic bout, her failure to take action was obvious.

She'd meant to break off the affair last Friday afternoon, but the moment that Eliot arrived, he'd started to kiss her. Then the hours had rushed by in such a fury of passion that she could summon neither breath nor will to give him notice. It had been like their first encounters, when she found herself astonished at his stamina and sensual imagination. Last Friday had been devoted to incandescent pleasure, and he'd been wise enough to say nothing about changing their very satisfactory arrangements.

This afternoon, he'd turned up in a lather, too. She loved how he was always so avid to have her.

Perhaps she should reconsider her plans to replace him. At least while desire still burned so hot. As she'd said to him, he was always as jumpy as a cat on a stove after seeing his father. The day that Eliot had suggested making their liaison public, he'd just endured a whole month under Deerforth's roof.

Then Eliot, plague take him, went and spoiled all her favorable thoughts by reaching across the tiny gap between them and curling his fingers around hers. Such a simple – such a chaste! – gesture, yet it shuddered through her like a blow. Verena offered her amours carnal pleasure. She didn't offer them anything that smacked of emotional connection.

But as, against her good judgement, she twined her hand around his, she could no longer deny that she was in trouble. After seven years of enjoyable adventures that hadn't come near to touching her heart, this affair with Eliot was different.

Terrifyingly different.

"I should get up and wash," she said, hearing the reluctance in her voice.

"Not yet," he said peacefully.

To the devil with her, she heeded his command and didn't move. Despite masculine commands being another thing that she'd banned from her life.

For an interval, they rested in silence. The panicked rush of Verena's blood slowed. Because while encouraging this closeness was the last thing she wanted, she couldn't deny that it was very pleasant to lie here, holding Eliot's hand while the waves of titanic pleasure ebbed.

Early sunset descended to deepen the coziness. The hour of his departure approached. That thought aroused a pang of regret, but she was so relaxed that she didn't even try to stifle it.

"Are you going out tonight?" he asked idly.

"Yes, there's some nonsense on at the Theatre Royal that everyone is talking about."

Verena couldn't summon much enthusiasm for the outing. She'd rather stay here with Eliot, who was one of the few people she knew who didn't expect her to glitter. She was rather tired of glittering, but it was what the world expected of brazen Verena Gerard.

How ironic that before she came to know him, she'd imagined Eliot sitting in perpetual judgement on her capricious ways. Yet he was the one person in her world who seemed content to let her be what she wanted to be.

"I saw it on Wednesday. You're right, it's nonsense, but amusing. You'll enjoy it."

Somehow she doubted it. "Are you going somewhere with Imogen?"

His sister had arrived in Town this week. While she found her feet in the ton, Eliot would accompany her in public. Later in the season, Verena supposed that he'd become more of a free agent, although he'd still escort Imogen to the most important events.

"Yes. Mrs. Bilson's ball is tonight." He didn't sound particularly eager to go out either.

"She's very pretty."

"Mrs. Bilson?"

After their exertions over the previous hours, Verena's puff of laughter was weary. "No, you fool. Imogen."

Two nights ago, Verena had seen the girl at the opera. She didn't look at all like Eliot. Instead, she was small and delicate, with porcelain white skin and masses of shining black hair.

"She'll make quite a splash," she said. "I imagine she'll be wed before the summer."

"Father is pushing a match with Lord Chippenham."

Horror flooded Verena. For once, the cause of her alarm wasn't her insidious and growing affection for Eliot. "Don't let it happen."

Eliot released her hand. She told herself that she didn't want to snatch it back, although she did.

"Why?" As he rose on one elbow to stare down at her, the drowsy languor seeped out of his gray eyes. "What do you know about him?"

Verena struggled to push away a raft of tormenting memories. "I haven't heard he's violent, if that's what's worrying you." Which didn't mean that he wasn't. "He's too old for her."

"Yes." Eliot studied her face.

She had an uncomfortable feeling that he saw more than she wanted him to. If he saw anything at all, it was more than she wanted him to. Verena still bore scars from her marriage, but she refused to wallow in self-pity. Not to mention that if she truly meant to break with Eliot, sharing confidences was self-defeating.

Nonetheless, the idea of that sweet child forced into an arranged match with an overbearing old man made her nauseous. "And he already has three children. The oldest girl must be close to the same age as Imogen."

Which promised a household poisoned with spite and jealousy, even if Imogen found her middle-aged bridegroom to her taste.

"Father wants Chippenham's support in parliament." As ever, when Eliot mentioned his father, his musical baritone went as flat as Lincolnshire fenland.

"What does Imogen want?"

To her surprise, a wry smile lengthened his mouth. "Imogen wants to go home and supervise the installation of a fountain in the south parterre at Hamble Park."

That surprised a laugh out of Verena. "She doesn't want a season?"

Eliot's expression softened. He loved his sister, something Verena both admired and envied. She had two older brothers. When she was a child, both of them had viewed her as an irrelevant nuisance. Since she'd run amok as a widow, neither of them had acknowledged her existence.

Imogen was lucky to have Eliot as a brother, although when it came to a loving parent, she was no luckier than Verena had been.

"So she says. At length. And she's not pleased with Father's marital schemes either."

"Good."

"I'm hoping she settles to staying in London until summer, though. At this stage, Father isn't pushing her too hard in Chippenham's direction, but he's spent a fortune on bringing her to Town. He's rented a house in Lorimer Square. He's bought her an extravagant wardrobe. He's planning a ball for her. Before he lets her throw all that away, he'll lock her in her room."

"As long as he doesn't beat her and starve her into submitting to his will."

When Eliot's gaze sharpened, Verena cursed the way that her tongue ran away with her. Before she could change the subject, he reached over to stroke her cheek. The tender touch slammed through her. How bizarre that such a gentle contact should have the power to stop her heart.

"Is that what happened to you?"

Her eyes flickered away, and she pulled free of his caress, pushing up against the pillows. The act of rejecting his concern wrenched at something inside her. The idea of leaning against Eliot and finding shelter in all that manly strength was too tempting. She really had to move on from him before she made a complete cake of herself.

"George Gerard wasn't an ideal match," she said with artificial carelessness, because the wretched truth was that her husband's cruelties haunted every minute of every day. "But it was a long time ago."

"Not that long." Eliot's concern didn't ease. "He had a reputation as a hard man on his servants and his horses and his dogs. I can't imagine he was any kinder to a wife."

Verena lay so stiff that her muscles ached. And stupidly, she felt the prickle of tears, when she'd stood dry-eyed beside her husband's deathbed.

She'd sworn then that the odious swine stretched out before her, struggling for his last breaths, would never make her shed another tear.

He'd died glaring his hatred but unable to voice a curse upon her head. She'd been glad, because the last words that she spoke to George were a promise to take every man in London into his ancestral bed and enjoy them in a way that she'd never enjoyed her spouse.

Now she didn't weep for her vile husband, but because of the gentleness in Eliot's voice. "Don't you dare feel sorry for me," she muttered. "I may have had a dreadful six years with George, but it's been nothing but gaiety and pleasure since."

Which was true. Although now that she'd taken Eliot as her lover, she couldn't help feeling that her frantic striving after forgetfulness held a touch of futility.

At twenty-three, she'd felt brave and daring when she launched her career as a wild widow. Even aside from discovering what a good lover could do for her, she'd so enjoyed knowing how George would loathe her profligacy. He'd once beaten her black and blue for smiling at a footman in a way he hadn't liked. Of course, he'd beaten her for other things, too. Every time some man shoved his cock deep inside Verena, the knowledge that she spat in the late Lord George's eye spiced her pleasure.

At thirty, she'd lost some of her gusto for new bedmates, although she continued to enjoy sexual relations. The men that she chose knew how to arouse a woman. On the rare occasion that she mistook a paramour's skill before inviting him to start an affair, he didn't last. She treated men like toys, entertaining while they were new, easy to cast away once she'd finished playing with them.

How she'd love to treat Eliot like a toy, too, but from the first, this liaison had taken her to places that she'd never been before. Places where the dashing, heartless, witty widow disappeared, and she caught a glimpse of the vulnerable girl that she'd been before her father and her husband had conspired to tame her.

Without success, she was proud to say.

Now she feared that Eliot Ridley might defeat her, when nobody else had. And he'd do it with kindness, which seemed even more ironic.

Eliot didn't react to her sudden spurt of temper. He was in general a calm man. Instead, he persisted in regarding her as if he saw right to her soul. Which was ridiculous, because she didn't have a soul.

What she had was a body that was hungry for carnal delight. In seven years, that hadn't changed. With Eliot, she was as greedy as she'd ever been. More.

"How could I feel sorry for you?" he said evenly. "You're magnificent."

Disbelief arched Verena's eyebrows. "Magnificent?"

"Yes, magnificent." He bent to kiss her. Despite the trouble that he caused her, she kissed him back. "Strong and invincible and beautiful."

At least he was no longer prying into the miseries of her marriage. Verena had no intention of allowing him to revive the subject.

She and Eliot were such different people. He was good to the bone, and she gloried in her sinfulness. But one thing they shared was an intense sexual appetite. If his touch had the power to dissolve her into a puddle of honey, hers turned him as hard as granite. When they'd first come together, his impressive virility had been a marvelous surprise.

He might be a saint, but he was a deuced potent one.

Verena knew just how to distract him from unwelcome questions. She curled her hand around the back of his neck and drew him down for another kiss, this one more purposeful. She used her tongue and teeth to tell him that the last thing she wanted to do right now was talk.

When his groan against her lips sounded like surrender, satisfaction flooded her. Even as her body softened and heated in preparation for a different kind of satisfaction.

It was a pity that her liaison with Eliot threatened to become too complicated. Because she was a long way from growing jaded with the magic that he conjured from her body.

Which only made her more desperate now.

Still kissing her, he rolled over and settled between her legs. He'd hardened fast. He always did. As a pleased little chuckle escaped her, one seeking hand reached down to test his readiness.

"Oh, lover," she sighed in anticipation. She squeezed him to spur him into action.

He wasn't quite ready to yield to her demands. Verena loved those encounters when they seemed to share a single mind as their bodies joined. She also loved it when sex turned into a continuation of a silent argument.

This was one of those occasions. She knew that Eliot wanted to discover more about her marriage, although Lord knew why. It wasn't an edifying story.

As he caught her hand and brought it to his lips, she felt the tension rise between them. Verena liked to maintain the advantage. She never quite managed it with Eliot, who for all his even temper and kindness, possessed an inner strength that awed her. He didn't rage and threaten and carry on like a child when he wanted his way. But once he set his sights on something, he was a determined opponent.

In his quiet way, he was the most formidable man that she'd ever known.

And dear God, he knew how to touch her. He slid down her body, tracing sizzling paths with his mouth. He took his time on her breasts. Eliot loved her breasts. He could bring her to orgasm playing with her nipples alone.

Today, he used his teeth until she was panting and writhing. But before she could slip over into rapture, he moved lower to bury his head between her legs.

Verena gave a choked growl of approval and raked her hand through the thick silk of his fair hair. He licked her cleft with a luxurious thoroughness that had her trembling anew. He caught her thighs and spread them wide, opening her for his wicked depredations.

Eliot took his time, concentrating on the pearl of flesh that sent lightning streaking through her. A liquid rush of pleasure overwhelmed her. She slammed over into a climax that had her seeing stars, then into another that left her quivering on a rack of pleasure.

As his tongue tormented her, he made low sounds of enjoyment. Her grip on his hair tightened as she spasmed again, then collapsed back against the sheets in exhaustion.

Her frantic grasp loosened to a fumbling caress. Every bone in her body had melted into syrup. She closed her eyes and struggled to fill her starving lungs.

Verena felt him move, then the sublime pleasure of his large, beautiful cock penetrating her. She was so wet that he slid into her with silky ease. She shifted to take him deeper, although he'd wrung every ounce of vigor from her when he pleased her with his mouth.

Oh, that mouth. The eighth wonder of the world.

Although perhaps the ninth, because he knew what to do with his dick, too.

Slow waves of pleasure lapped over her, as he adopted a driving rhythm as powerful as the tides. By the time he withdrew, she was quaking with another climax. Through half-open eyes, she watched him sit up and grab for a towel from the bedside table.

She loved to observe his face when he found his bliss. The skin clung to those perfect bones, and his eyes became opaque and distant. It was as if this private Eliot was hers alone.

Verena lifted a hand that felt like it weighed a ton and laid it on his thigh, feeling his release vibrate under her palm. "Thank you," she said, her voice thick. "That was glorious."

He wiped himself off and cast the crumpled towel to the floor. "Yes, it was."

When he leaned down to kiss her, she was too weary to inject much passion into her response. The salty flavour of his lips reminded her of how his mouth had sent her flying up beyond the clouds.

Raising his head, he smiled down at her. "I really must go. It's late."

The room had grown dim and shadowy, the only light coming from the fire. She should light some candles. "I'd offer you dinner, but I need to dress for the theater."

Where she'd meet people she didn't care about and watch a play that held no interest. She'd rather stay here with Eliot. The thought conveyed an odious tinge of domesticity, but she was too well pleasured to summon her usual prickly reaction.

"I can't let Imogen down, and the Bilsons have invited us to dine first." Despite what he said, he remained propped on one elbow, studying her. "I'll see you next Friday."

"Yes," she said and heard the regret in her voice. Friday seemed an age away. "I'm sure our paths will cross during the week."

When they'd pretend to be strangers. It was one of the inconveniences of this affair. Her other lovers had all been as disreputable as she was, but Eliot needed to maintain his good name. Even more so, now that he helped his sister to navigate her first season.

He left the bed and walked with that long graceful prowl toward the dressing room where he'd wash and dress. Verena lay exactly where she was, enjoying the sight of those firm buttocks clenching and releasing with each step. Long scratches scored his back. When he left to hobnob with people who despised her, he'd bear her secret mark. That was a thrill that never failed.

Eliot lingered in the doorway and glanced back with a piercing light in his gray eyes. "That was splendid, Verena. But don't imagine that sex will always allow you to dodge questions you don't want to answer."

Before she could summon an adequate response, he disappeared into the dressing room.

CHAPTER FOUR

The Lumsden ball was held in their magnificent mansion in Lorimer Square. It was always accounted one of the highlights of the London season. This year, the event was more spectacular than usual, because it also served as the official launch for their daughter Harriet Comerford.

Verena stood with Celia and Freddie Edgecombe and fanned herself idly, as she studied the Comerford chit. Pretty. Blonde. Lively. She was already acclaimed as a diamond of the first water. The Lumsdens should have no trouble marrying her off in style.

Harriet was great friends with Eliot's sister Imogen. Down in the wilds of Gloucestershire, the Lumsdens and Ridleys were neighbours. The two girls were inseparable, although at this moment, when Verena glanced around the ballroom, Imogen was nowhere to be seen.

The rest of her family was present, though. Near the French doors, Deerforth was holding forth on some topic dear to his heart to a clearly bored Lady Tierney. The mousy cousin was here somewhere, too, Verena was sure. After dancing with Elizabeth Tierney, Eliot was escorting her back to her mother, which might offer that lady some relief from Deerforth.

Elizabeth Tierney was as pretty as Lily Bilson. Another girl who would make Eliot an excellent wife, which must explain why Verena wanted to scratch the little poppet's big blue eyes out.

She really must do something to control her murderous impulses toward this year's crop of debutantes.

"Who are you engaged to partner for the next dance?" Celia asked her a few minutes later.

"Your husband," Verena said with a smile. She turned to Freddie. "My lord, shall we proceed?"

"With pleasure."

As Freddie held out his hand, a deep voice spoke from behind her. "I believe this is my dance."

Shock and unwelcome pleasure rippled through Verena. She turned slowly to meet Eliot's steady gray gaze. As was always the case when she encountered him in public, his expression was all cool composure. Only she saw the fire blazing in his silvery eyes.

"Lord Colville, I don't recall you asking me." Because he hadn't, the rogue. The reckless rogue, which was something she'd never thought to call him before this. "I promised this dance to Lord Edgecombe."

Freddie, who was twenty years older than Eliot and half a foot shorter, cast Eliot an uncertain glance and let his hand drop to his side. Eliot, as ever, was all that was polite, but his air of determination hinted that he had no intention of retreating.

"We arranged things yesterday in the park. I'm devastated that you don't remember, my lady."

She narrowed her eyes on him. They'd exchanged a few words in Hyde Park during the fashionable hour, but they hadn't ventured beyond pleasantries. He'd certainly never warned her that he intended to risk dancing with her under society's gaze. "As I don't recall that conversation, and Lord Edgecombe has—"

"Verena, I've danced with you already tonight," Freddie said with a cheery lack of chivalry that she couldn't help but resent. "If there's been a mix-up, I'm happy to yield to Colville's claim on this occasion." He beamed, as if he'd sorted everything out to general satisfaction.

Which was far from true.

Verena bit back an irritated response. Celia's inquisitive stare made the hair prickle on the back of her neck.

"Thank you, Edgecombe. Very gentlemanly of you." Eliot extended his gloved hand. "My lady?"

The orchestra played the introduction to summon the dancers to the floor. It had to be a waltz, didn't it? Verena smoothed out her expression, although inside she was fuming. Didn't Eliot realize that this mad gesture put seven months of hard-won discretion in jeopardy?

When she met his eyes, he smiled at her, which made her want to hit him with her fan. Or something heavier, like a club, if only she could lay hands on one. The ballroom was sadly lacking in suitable weaponry.

Any further objections to partnering Eliot would only draw more attention. So she plastered a smile on her face and took his hand. "Then I accept with pleasure, my lord."

Was she alone in noting the wolfish satisfaction that lit Lord Colville's face? It was a very un-Eliot expression. At least in public.

"Excellent." His fingers curled around hers, and even through two layers of gloves, she felt a zing of heat. She might be annoyed with him, but that didn't lessen the animal attraction raging between them.

She didn't speak, as he led her out onto the dance floor and put his arm around her waist. Over his black-clad shoulder, Verena saw Lord Deerforth shoot them a disapproving glare. He would consider Verena an unsuitable partner for his much-admired son. A faint whisper rose above the music. She and Eliot had never waltzed together before. The pairing would strike the ton as bizarre. And infernally interesting.

"You're creating a spectacle," she hissed under her breath, as she set her other hand on his shoulder. "What on earth are you up to, you lunatic?"

His smile didn't falter. "I'm dancing with the woman I want to hold in my arms. It isn't a crime."

The music turned to a lilting melody, and she and Eliot began to move in time. "It mightn't be a crime, but it's certainly a mistake."

He glanced down at her, and as ever, the warmth in his eyes made her silly heart squeeze tight and flip over. "It doesn't feel like a mistake."

"It will in the morning, when the world is gossiping about the saint and the sinner, and your political backers are asking themselves whether you're really such an upright character after all, or whether I've managed to corrupt you."

"It's a dance, Verena. I'm not copulating with you in full view of the beau monde. You're overreacting."

She scowled. "No, I'm not. Because now that we've danced together, people will start to speculate about what else we might do together."

"I can cope with a bit of talk." He kept smiling, plague take him. "I'm sick of other people setting the agenda for my life."

They might be conducting a furious argument in murmurs, but the physical compatibility that produced such fireworks in bed held true here, too. She felt like their bodies moved as one. Freddie Edgecombe danced like an arthritic cart horse. Her toes at least appreciated Eliot's bold invitation.

"So you're setting the agenda for my life instead." The dangerous sweetness in her tone should warn him of her displeasure. But then, he was aware of that already, wasn't he? He was the most perceptive man she knew, and she wasn't doing much to conceal her crankiness.

"You're making too much of this," he said lightly. "Although if you don't start looking just a tad happier, you really will have people asking questions about what we mean to each other."

He was right, to blazes with him. She might be lecturing him on decorum, but she was doing very little to maintain it.

Verena sucked in a tattered breath and struggled to restore an appearance of long-suffering boredom. It was harder than it should be. What she wanted most of all was a chance to give Eliot a good shake. She could weather a little – or a lot – of gossip. After all, she was already the notorious widow. But Eliot had a reputation to uphold. Not only that, his sister was on the marriage mart this season. His behavior mattered even more than usual.

It was odd, and surely a figment of her imagination, but as she drew breath, she caught Eliot's spicy scent. He was holding her at a proper distance, and the overheated air was sickly with the perfumes the women wore and the fragrance of wilting hothouse flowers. Not to mention a good dose of upper-class perspiration.

Her senses were so attuned to Eliot that the drift of male musk set her pulses racing. In the last six months, that rich scent had become the aroma of paradise.

A purely private paradise.

"What in Hades do you hope to achieve with these antics?" Her voice remained stony, despite the forbidden longing that found a home inside her.

Still he smiled, the scoundrel. She wanted to kick him in the shin and remind him that she wasn't a fit partner. It was the smile that he gave her when they were alone and nobody was watching. It was the smile that told her he judged Verena Gerard to be the most marvelous being in creation and he knew how lucky he was to hold her in his arms.

Even in private, that smile always made her skin itch. Partly because it made her nitwit heart flutter like a trapped linnet in a cage. Here, where hundreds of eyes focused on their unlikely pairing, it betrayed far too much about his penchant for the naughty widow.

"Antics? I'm a gentleman dancing with a lady at a society event. All perfectly acceptable."

Except it wasn't, and he knew it. Imogen waltzed past in the arms of Anthony Comerford, the Lumsdens' oldest son. As she stared at her brother, her features were vivid with curiosity. She'd been in Town a mere fortnight, and already she'd heard of the wild and willful Lady Verena, it seemed.

"Stop looking at me like that," she muttered, struggling to maintain her pretense at ennui. Eliot might have lost his mind, but she could still do her best to convey an air of distance.

"How am I looking at you?"

Her eyes narrowed again, then very deliberately she glanced over his shoulder and nodded at Shelburn, who was dancing with

Elizabeth Tierney. The devil had the temerity to wink at her and shake his head in theatrical commiseration at her incompatible partner.

If only he knew how compatible she and Eliot in fact were. Physically at least. But of course, she didn't want Shelburn to know that. She didn't want anyone to know that.

"Like I'm a chocolate éclair, and you're a man with a taste for good pastry."

His low laugh vibrated under the hand that she'd placed on his shoulder. She might be annoyed with Eliot. She *was* annoyed with Eliot. But that rumble of a laugh always sent pleasure rippling through her. Tonight was no different, although she heartily wished that it was.

"That's just how I feel."

She'd very much like to tug at the crisp golden curls at his nape to bring him back to reality. But if she did, it would look like a caress. Verena tried to stiffen and pull back, but the hand at her waist wouldn't budge.

Most of her lovers did her bidding. She'd learned early in their affair that Eliot had a mind of his own. However much he desired her, she'd never managed to turn him into a lapdog. "How much longer will this pestilential waltz last?"

He laughed again. Her ill humor didn't seem to depress his spirits at all. "Long enough."

"I'd like to sit down."

"No, you wouldn't."

No, she wouldn't. Because despite her worry and fluster and irritation, waltzing with Eliot was like flying.

Verena had always loved to dance, ever since her first season. She rarely had a partner to match her, though. Eliot was just right, so that she became part of the music, a feather floating around the room without her feet touching the ground.

It was a pity that they were arguing. It was a pity that they would never dance together again. Eliot was the best dance partner that she'd ever had.

The devil was the best lover that she'd ever had. It was even more of a pity that the affair had to end. He was becoming reckless, and she couldn't bear the thought of his association with her causing him lasting harm.

"Smile, Verena. The éclair is glaring at me as if it's got murder on its mind."

He performed a dizzying circle and when he reversed direction, they'd edged closer. The evocative smell of his skin made her head swim, even without taking account of the whirling movements of the waltz. His hand was warm at her waist and made her wish that he was touching naked skin. The layers of his glove and her silk gown and all the petticoats beneath were an annoyance. She fixed her gaze on his snowy white neckcloth and reminded herself that she was angry with him.

"The éclair does," she retorted, to her relief hearing the music proceed to the coda. The dance was nearly done, thank goodness. She could go back to showing the world that Eliot Ridley meant nothing to her.

He tightened his hold and sidestepped with a grace that under different circumstances, she might have admired. Too quickly for her to realize his strategy, let alone do anything to stop him, she found herself twirling into a corridor leading off the ballroom.

"Eliot, what the devil game are you playing?" she asked, as she realized that they were now alone.

He stopped moving but kept hold of her. "I want to talk to you."

She wanted to talk to him, too, to ring a peal over that handsome head and remind him of what was at stake in keeping their affair secret. But she remained conscious that they were in public. He seemed to have forgotten that. How the ton would laugh to know that right now, the bold widow counseled caution, while the saint tested the rules of propriety.

"Anything you say can wait until Friday," she snapped, pushing back on the hand on her waist. But Eliot was in a commanding mood. That chiseled jaw was set in adamant lines. Even more than usual, he looked like Galahad resolved to seize the Grail.

Despite the promptings of good sense – and whatever her flighty reputation, Verena possessed her share of practical intelligence – she couldn't suppress a reluctant thrill at how masterful he was. If they'd been on their own, she'd have melted into his arms and begged him to take her hard.

But that was the problem, wasn't it? They weren't on their own. Although when he ushered her down the corridor and into a small salon, they were as unobserved as a crowded ball permitted.

The hand on her arm was implacable as he shut the door behind him. Sconces lit the room. It wasn't bright, but there was enough light for Verena to make out Eliot's urgent expression and the muscle flickering in his cheek.

He'd kept up his urbane manner when he danced with her and fended off her demands to cease this outlandish behavior. There was nothing urbane about the man who now faced her down. He looked like he'd reached the limit of his patience. What on earth was wrong with him?

"Yes, I can wait until Friday if I have to." His voice wasn't that easy musical baritone either. It was rough with intense emotion.

As she pulled away, she frowned. "Eliot, what are you doing?"

She wasn't even sure that he heard her question. He flattened his elegant hands against the gleaming wood of the door, and the expression in his eyes scalded her. His behavior all night had unsettled her, worried her. But as she stared into his taut features, for the first time, she was afraid.

Because for seven months, she'd tried to ignore the tensions between them. Right now, she had a sick feeling that those tensions had reached breaking point. Eliot certainly looked as if he was close to shattering.

It was colder in the small room than it was in the overcrowded ballroom. But the chill that iced Verena's blood had nothing to do with the spring night.

His voice vibrated with feeling as he went on. "But aren't you sick of always having to wait until Friday? Aren't you sick of squashing our real life into a couple of hours a week, then spending the rest of our days barely surviving on a word here and there? A few moments as partners in the line of a dance? A glimpse across a crowded room with a silent message that neither of us can acknowledge? Don't you feel like you're starving to death, Verena?"

Dear God, he really was going to smash everything. She supposed that she should be pleased. If he kept going like this, she'd have the perfect excuse for sending him away.

She wasn't pleased. She was devastated to think that all the joy between them came to a bitter end.

Licking dry lips, she backed away another step. A shaking hand lifted to where her heart raced as if it tried to escape the confines of her chest. "We decided when we came together that we'd keep our liaison secret."

He straightened, and his glare cut through all the comfortable delusions that she'd wrapped around herself for more than half a year. Comfortable delusions that had threatened to strangle her as the weeks went on. "Then I'm deciding now that it's not enough."

"You have a political career and a family to consider." She struggled to sound as if she had some control here.

"Compared to what I feel for you, I don't give a rat's arse about either."

"You must. Imogen—"

"Imogen is pretty and rich, and far from convinced that she's ready to marry anyway. She'll do perfectly well for herself, whatever scandal her brother causes."

Shocked, Verena studied his expression. "You don't mean that."

"Yes, I do."

Yes, he did. She had no doubt that he was in earnest. "What about wanting to be prime minister?"

"Fuck that, too."

She felt the blood drain from her face. Eliot rarely used strong language in front of her. He mightn't be the plaster saint that she'd once called him, but at heart he was a gentleman.

Verena scrambled for some way to head off the disaster that she saw rushing toward her. "We can...we can meet on a second afternoon each week. Even three."

Although the more often that he called, the greater the likelihood of discovery. On the other hand, the thought of having Eliot in her bed several times a week was appealing.

Too appealing.

"Fuck that as well," he grated out. "Don't you understand, Verena? We've gone past the point where a few hours here or there are enough. I love you."

Her breath stopped. Her heart stopped. By heaven, time itself stopped.

He loved her?

The room and everything in it faded to a gray mist. Even Eliot's face became a blur.

"Eliot..." she forced out through a throat that felt like it was lined with broken glass.

Surging forward, he fell to one knee before her. He grabbed her shaking hand and kept hold of it, despite her frantic attempts to pull free. "Verena, I love you, and I want to make you my wife. Will you marry me, my darling?"

CHAPTER FIVE

*E*liot wasn't a stupid man. He knew that Verena was skittish on the subject of marriage. Even to someone she liked.

She was reluctant to entrust herself to a man. Why shouldn't she be? Her life offered a freedom that few women ever enjoyed. And hers was such a vivid, untamed spirit.

Not to mention that even before he came to her bed, he'd guessed that her first marriage had been a catastrophe. Her randy old goat of a husband had never been discreet about his dalliances, and there were also nasty rumors about the late Lord George Gerard's taste for violence.

Eliot could cope without hearing an immediate and unconditional yes in answer to his proposal. It would be an uphill battle to convince her that they had a future together. But while for months, he'd told himself that he could live with what little she gave him, it wasn't enough. He was ready to take the next step in life, and he wanted to take that step with Verena.

"Say something, sweetheart," he said, trying to muster a smile, but failing miserably. He stared up at her from where he was kneeling and prayed that this wasn't turning into a complete debacle.

Her throat moved as she swallowed. She'd gone as pale as paper, and not even the most optimistic fellow could read anything except utter horror in her expression.

This was his first attempt at a proposal. It was clear that he needed more practice.

She swallowed again. "Are you completely mad?"

"It's not mad to want to marry you."

"Yes, it is. For pity's sake, why would you even think of such a thing?"

He frowned. "Because I love you. And I want to treat you with honor. And I'm bloody sick of sneaking around, as if I'm committing some crime by wanting you."

She jerked free and retreated to the far wall. If she could go even further away, he knew she would. As far as Tahiti, if she could. "We're having an affair."

"It's not enough."

"It has to be."

Feeling absurd on his knees, Eliot struggled to his feet. His grand romantic gesture had fallen flat. He hadn't expected Verena to agree to marry him. Not at first. But he hadn't expected this level of resistance.

He told himself that her reaction shouldn't sting. After all, however uninhibited she was with her body, she'd always guarded her emotions behind high stone walls. "I've never been so happy in my life as I've been since we came together. Haven't you been happy with me?"

She still had that strange, numb look on her face. Then he watched her gather herself together and straighten. Her delicate jaw set with the stubbornness that he recognized. When her voice emerged, it was cold and mocking. "You've been...amusing."

She'd sounded like that when they first met. She still sounded like that, when some gentleman overreached the bounds of good manners. As they occasionally did when they'd heard too much gossip about her promiscuity, without taking into consideration how selective she was when she took a lover.

Eliot hid a wince. Never had he imagined that she'd greet his declaration of love with that cutting tone. "Is that all?"

"That's all I ask of a lover." She twined her hands in front of her. Then, as though afraid of betraying her inner turmoil, she let her hands drop to her sides.

He squared his shoulders. He wasn't sorry that he'd told her of his love. He wasn't sorry that he'd asked her to marry him. But by God, he was sorry that he'd upset her. Standing there in all her finery, she looked brittle enough to shatter into a thousand tiny pieces.

During these last months, he'd been living a lie, and he wasn't a man who thrived on deceit. That endless month in the country had given him time to think about what he wanted from life. In essence that boiled down to one thing.

Verena.

Who, it seemed, didn't want him. At least in the until death do them part sense.

"This is all my fault." She licked her lips again and went on in that crystalline voice he hated. "I owe you an apology."

Every instinct warned Eliot that he wouldn't like what was coming. "Oh?"

He wasn't fool enough to hope that she meant to relent. Her exquisite features could be carved from ice. That wasn't the face of a woman about to give her suitor a joyful acceptance.

"I've had it in mind for a while that our liaison has run its course. I should have spoken up weeks ago."

The room went dark. Eliot felt like he staggered, although when he came back to himself, he remained standing in front of her.

"You want to finish with me?" The quaking agony in his voice made him cringe.

"Yes," she said, as if she spoke to a stranger. "If I'd mentioned my intentions earlier, it might have saved us both this current embarrassment."

Eliot took a grip on his rising anger, although he had less success controlling the great rivers of pain rolling through him and threatening to drown him. "But we still want each other."

He waited for her to deny that, while he wondered how he'd been so utterly wrong about her feelings. The last time they were together, she'd been like fire in his arms. Every time they were together, she met him with a desire that matched his own. The mighty passion they shared was the stuff that shook empires.

Or so he'd believed.

Verena shrugged, as if what she said didn't slice a great jagged rift across his heart. "You're an excellent lover. However that is no longer the issue. I've enjoyed our association, but it's over. We've been together more than half a year. There's nothing new to discover."

His eyes narrowed on her. Now that his immediate shock receded, something about her callous response didn't ring true. "I haven't noticed any signs of boredom. Not a single yawn, in fact."

She looked startled, as though she hadn't expected him to come back fighting. "Don't make this any more difficult than it needs to be."

Eliot was still hurt, he was still furious. But his excellent mind had started to work again, and there was more going on here, other than a lady casting off a disagreeable swain. He suddenly recalled that her immediate reaction to his proposal, before she had a chance to mask her feelings, hadn't been distaste. It had been fear. "Perhaps I need to make this so difficult that you'll change your mind."

She shook her head. "You have too much pride to become a pest."

His short laugh conveyed no genuine amusement. "You mistake me, my lady. Where you're concerned, I have no pride at all."

He caught another flash of emotion in her extraordinary blue eyes. More fear? Why the hell would she be frightened? They'd been intimate for six months. She must know that he'd never hit a woman.

But George Gerard had.

"I'm sorry to hear that." Her voice lost its frozen edge, lowered to persuasion. "Think, Eliot! You've tried like the devil to avoid scandal. And while you say that you don't care about your family, I know you do. If we shake hands and part now, nobody need ever know that angelic Viscount Colville strayed over into an imprudent flirtation with that hussy Verena Gerard. You can go on to a great political career, Imogen can enjoy a brilliant season, and I can select my next lover without having to check behind me to see if you're making a nuisance of yourself. Surely that's a better outcome than you kicking up a fuss to no purpose."

Only one part of that vile little recital stuck in his mind. "Your next lover?"

She waved to indicate that he quibbled about trivialities. "Why not my next lover? Did you imagine you'd spoiled me for any other man? You're good, my lord. But you're not that good."

Eliot sucked in a ragged breath. His temper had subsided. He was still in pain, but he'd survive. He even felt a faint twinge of hope that he prayed wasn't just wishful thinking. Because Verena was trying too hard to make him march out in a huff. "You've spoiled me for any other woman."

For a moment, the careless, disdainful façade cracked. He caught a glimpse of a devastation to match his own. Then she gathered her composure about her and returned to acting like a stern goddess spurning an unworthy acolyte.

But it was too late. He'd seen enough to know that while his plan to claim her as his might be ambitious, it wasn't impossible. She cared about him. More than she wanted to.

Not that he underestimated Verena's powerful will, or how she set that will against him.

Her expression turned cynical. "You'll get over it."

He found it in him to smile at her as if she was the sun in his sky. Why not? She was. "Never."

Her lush lips flattened. "Then you have untold misery to look forward to."

Eliot frowned. "Only a few minutes ago, you offered to give me a couple of extra afternoons a week. That doesn't sit well with a request never to darken your door again."

A hunted expression crossed Verena's face. Any doubts that she wanted him to throw a tantrum and flounce out faded. "I felt sorry for you."

This time, his laugh held a note of genuine humor. "Did you indeed?"

She looked startled and tried to retreat further, but she was already on the edge of the room. "Yes."

He arched mocking eyebrows. "So that's why you offered to spend more time with me, just before you sent me on my way forever?"

"Yes."

He folded his arms over his chest to stop himself from grabbing her and kissing her until she saw reason. Right now, she was in no mood to capitulate. "That makes no sense."

"It doesn't matter if it does or not." When she at last stepped forward, he wasn't surprised. Retreat wasn't Verena's style. It was one of the many things that he admired about her. "I owe you nothing. You don't own me. I choose who shares my bed, and from now on, I choose to deny you a place there."

"You have the right to do that."

He'd caught her off guard again. The frosty mask slipped once more, as she regarded him uncertainly. "Then you accept that the affair is over?"

"I accept that the way things have been is no longer how they should continue."

Verena frowned. She was smart enough to know that he might sound like he was cooperating, but there was a catch. "I'm glad. For a moment there, I was worried you meant to behave like a fool."

"I'm no fool, Verena," he responded with a rasp. "So don't play me for one."

"I hope we can part without bitterness." When he didn't reply, she ventured closer. "Now, let me go back to the ballroom."

"Where we act like strangers?"

She stared hard at him. For the first time, he couldn't pretend that she didn't mean what she said when she tried to end the affair. She was frightened enough to run away from something that promised to be extraordinary. It proved how his proposal had panicked her. "I have a strong suspicion that all round, it would be better if we'd stayed strangers from the beginning, Eliot."

He'd never believe that, no matter what agony he suffered now. Until he met Verena, he'd only been half alive. The ghastly prospect of going back to that colorless existence steeled his purpose. "Will you kiss me goodbye?"

Another flash of fear, although this time she held her ground. "No."

"That's not very generous."

She responded with irritated bewilderment. "I have a dreadful feeling that you're not taking me seriously."

He shrugged. "Our affair is over. I understand."

Puzzled eyes focused on him. But he hadn't spent his adult life in politics without learning to hide his thoughts from an opponent. Right now, this woman he loved more than his life had become his opponent.

"Then let me go."

Never.

With exaggerated politeness, he stepped aside from the door. "You're free, Verena."

She didn't move to leave straightaway, which at least confirmed one of his hunches. The dread that she tried so hard to hide didn't stem from fear of violence. She knew that he'd never hurt her. At least physically. Emotionally was another story.

Did his love threaten her emotional independence? Was that why she sent him away? Or was that just more wishful thinking?

"I am. And I intend to stay that way." Her voice was hard, but at least she sounded like herself again and not some horrid puppet.

He bowed his head in acknowledgement. "I have no intention of curtailing your freedom."

"Of course you don't." Her smile conveyed sour agreement. "You just want to marry me."

Eliot sent her a direct look. She was so strong, yet so fragile. Her strength was like fine Venetian glass. One careless touch, and she'd fracture into jagged shards. If she truly meant to give him his marching orders, it hadn't made her happy. She looked as if she'd snap into pieces if he spoke one harsh word.

Verena would hate that vulnerability. She accused him of being proud, but he wasn't, not really. She however had only survived because of her pride. He tried to imagine how her late husband's contemptuous treatment had wounded that pride.

Eliot already knew that he was paying the price for another man's sins. That bastard George Gerard might be cold in his grave, but the harm he'd done lived on. Would it live on forever?

Eliot's voice was low and sincere, as he studied this woman he adored. He hoped that she heard him. He hoped that she hadn't moved so far away that he could no longer reach her. All he could do was trust in the intimacy that they'd established through half a year of breathtaking pleasure.

"You can be free when you're with another person, Verena, if it's the right person. You can be a prisoner all on your own, if an unhappy past holds you in its grip. My love doesn't include a need to cage you or contain you. I love your wildness. I love your spirit. I want a woman who will challenge me and enchant me and meet me as an equal. I believe that woman is you."

She went even paler, but to his regret, showed no sign of softening. "Then you're mistaken," she said in a steady voice.

"I don't accept that."

"You will."

She swept forward, passing so close that he caught a trace of sensual jasmine perfume. The idea that he'd never hold her close again and breathe in that heady fragrance made him shut his eyes in anguish.

He heard the click of the door. When he opened his eyes, Verena was gone.

Verena's legs were shaking, as she made her way along the corridor toward the crowded ballroom. A quadrille was in progress, and the cheerful music jangled against her screaming nerves. What she'd like more than anything was to order her carriage and go home. Then indulge in a good, long cry.

But something in her knew that if she did, it would mean Eliot scored a point against her. She couldn't bear that, even if she felt like she'd just come through a brutal battle. A battle that she suspected she'd emerged from as the battered loser. Despite the fact that she'd finally broken with Eliot, and she was the one who had walked away and left him standing bereft.

She, on the other hand, had regained her independence. Now she was ready to start looking for her new lover. Most of the time, this was something she enjoyed. Before she made her choice and took a man to her bed, she felt such delicious anticipation. Even if the lover didn't live up to expectations in the end, there was a thrill in imagining that he might.

To hell with Eliot Ridley. Before their affair, she'd lived a life of endless excitement, packed with novelty and adventure. How right she'd been to fear the harm her time with Eliot might do to that headstrong, unruly creature. She'd stayed too long with him, allowed herself to grow comfortable. Despite the breathless passion of their sexual encounters, there had been an ease between them that held almost a hint of the domestic. When domesticity was something that sparkling, wayward Verena Gerard would never again countenance.

Plague take him, Eliot had made her dull and contented and biddable, like a well-fed cow in a rich green field. She'd allowed herself to sink into an unthinking happiness that threatened everything she'd made of herself during these last hectic years. She'd sworn that no man would ever fence her in again. Yet with Eliot, she'd all but put her head into the halter and invited him to lead her into the barn.

A chill rippled through her as she recalled the last time that a male had claimed any authority over her. And he'd done it with the sanction of church and society, because he bore the title of husband. Since George's death, an occasional lover had dared to make demands. The affair had ended there and then. Verena Gerard was her own woman and took direction from no man, by God.

Not that Eliot had ever given her orders. He was too subtle for that, the weasel.

No, he'd let her come to him and offer her allegiance. Now the fool imagined that she'd make him a fine wife. If she wasn't so upset, she'd almost laugh at the picture of notorious Verena Gerard as a political hostess. The world would certainly laugh.

She was glad that their affair was over and she'd never lie in his arms again. She was so glad, she was bloody ecstatic.

When a choked sob rose in her throat, she forced it back. She clenched her hands into fists in her dark purple skirts, as she fought the urge to dissolve into a storm of tears. Here, where any betrayal of emotion would have the ton's gossips agog to witness that Lady Verena was just as vulnerable as any other feeble woman.

No man would make her cry in public. That was too pathetic, and she'd never be pathetic again.

How dare Eliot propose? As if she had any intention of dwindling into a mere wife. She was spectacular Verena Gerard, who had London at her feet. Or at least the part of London that wasn't prissy and proper and shocked that a woman should enjoy the same freedoms as a man.

How dare Eliot—

"Verena?"

The sound of her name had her blinking away tears and plastering a smile to her face. When she was married to George, she'd learned to smile through disaster. That carefree, superior smile had defended her against all the curiosity and spite.

Nobody could pity her or laugh at her or despise her when they saw that she took life as a great joke. That smile had carried her through her unbearable marriage and had helped her to become the glittering queen of a sensual realm. That smile expressed every ounce of dominion that she'd wrung from a life where she'd once been hurt and frightened and alone and helpless.

Damn it, she hadn't felt helpless since George died. Until tonight, when Eliot had told her that he loved her.

"Are you all right? You're looking rather on edge." The baritone voice addressing her from the doorway to the ballroom was smooth and deep. Best of all, it didn't belong to Eliot Ridley.

She guessed her former paramour remained in that small room, coming to terms with her rejection.

What a price he'd pay, if she'd been mutton-headed enough to say yes. He'd lose everything that he'd worked for. In return for what? A woman derided as a trollop. A woman who had already proven a miserable failure at married life.

Eliot didn't love her, not really. How could he? That heartfelt declaration was just more lunacy.

"Not at all." She kept her smile in place as she strolled toward Shelburn. "I just needed a little air."

She tried to sound like her insouciant self. Shelburn's frown told her that she might be failing at that. "It's our dance. Or would you rather sit this one out?"

She had a reputation for glittering at social events. By all that was holy, she'd glitter at this one. Or she might as well give up and admit that George was right when he'd called her a tedious little creature, of interest to nobody who possessed a scrap of discernment.

"Sit it out? To Hades with that idea." She leveled her shoulders and marched forward with her hand extended. She was proud to see that it didn't even tremble, despite the whirlpool of emotion churning inside her. "Let's show the world how it's done, my lord."

CHAPTER SIX

E liot pulled his elegant yellow curricle to a stop in front of Verena's house on Half Moon Street. Tom, his tiger, slid off the back and ran forward to hold the horses, who tossed their heads and snorted and did their best to give the impression that standing still was beneath their dignity.

The grays were a recent purchase. They were spectacular to look at, but Eliot still needed to get their measure.

After jumping down from the carriage, he mounted the short flight of steps to Verena's door two at a time. Merton responded to his sharp knock with his usual lack of reaction and left him to cool his heels in the hall.

The butler was used to seeing him on a Friday, although on those occasions, Eliot came in through the back garden, and he'd missed calling on Verena last week. Staying away had been deuced difficult, but he'd been too raw after she ended their affair to face another argument.

That was ten days ago. He'd hoped that she'd since had a chance to reconsider her decision. He'd hoped that she might contact him to say she'd welcome seeing him again. He wasn't optimistic enough to imagine that she might write to say she'd decided to marry him.

To his regret, there had been no note from Half Moon Street.

He'd missed her like the very devil. At a couple of social events, he'd glimpsed her from a distance. She hadn't acknowledged him, and he had a feeling that she'd arranged things so that they didn't partner each other in the line of a dance. Several times, he'd approached to request a waltz, but she'd proven elusive. Not only had she proven elusive, she'd seemed determined to flirt with every dim-witted rogue in London.

Eliot tried to tell himself that she'd flirted at public events throughout their affair. If she hadn't, people might wonder what had changed. The fact that she'd apparently just spent six months without a lover had excited enough questions.

But that had been back when he'd known that he held her interest. Now she might be looking for someone to fill his place in her bed.

Over his dead body.

He'd even started attending the kind of events that he often avoided, gatherings that were a little too outré for debutantes. As luck would have it, Imogen had been at a country house party for most of last week, so he hadn't had to escort her anywhere respectable. His appearance at a few less respectable balls had caused comment, he knew, but he was more interested in getting Verena back than in preserving his reputation as a proper young fellow.

He'd awaited a summons from his father, who wouldn't approve of Eliot's recent taste for low company. But it turned out that Lord Deerforth wasn't thinking about his son. Instead, he was distracted by hopes of Imogen's visit to Lord Halston's estate resulting in a proposal.

Eliot wasn't convinced that the elusive Earl of Halston was contemplating marriage. His sister was pretty and lively, but she didn't strike Eliot as the girl to steal the rake's heart.

But then, the heart was mysterious territory. Who would have thought that ambitious Eliot Ridley would be more than happy to throw away his political plans, once he fell headlong in love with free-spirited Verena Gerard?

Free-spirited Verena Gerard, who had danced with every blockhead in the ton over the last ten days. Every blockhead apart from Eliot Ridley.

Their awareness of each other had always approached the uncanny. Now Verena was using that awareness against him.

She was avoiding him.

So far, he had let her get away with that. But no longer.

Eliot didn't expect her to take him back into her bed today – although he'd sing hallelujahs if she did. But he wanted to talk to her. A drive in the park would reassure her that they were on neutral territory when he stated his case.

He used the military term deliberately.

Right now, he couldn't help viewing his courtship as a war. As the time between his arrival and her appearance lengthened, his hopes of emerging the victor from this particular battle faded with every minute. He reminded himself that losing one battle didn't mean losing the war. This would be a long campaign. A retreat today just signaled a need to refine his strategy.

But, dear God, how it hurt to be here in this house where he'd passed the happiest hours of his life and feel so unwelcome. He hoped to hell that

Verena came around to his way of thinking before too long, or he'd be a broken man.

Eliot heard a light step on the staircase. Despite everything, his heart rose in pleasure as Verena descended to the tiled floor. Pleasure, and relief strong enough to trap the breath in his lungs.

After not speaking to her in days, he starved for the sight of her. Smiling with the appreciation that not even their estrangement could crush, he stood and bowed. "Good afternoon, Verena."

No smile in return. As she tugged on a stylish pair of red leather gloves, her movements were spiky with irritation. "Eliot, what in heaven's name are you doing here?"

She didn't sound pleased to see him. He hadn't thought that she would be. Nonetheless, the edge to her tone made him stiffen. "It's Friday."

Her eyebrows arched with the insolence that had stolen his heart the day they'd met. Her spirit had always challenged his. Never more so than now, when she clearly wished him to perdition. "There's one in every week I believe."

"Your Fridays are mine."

Her lips turned down. "They might have been, once upon a time. Thank you for returning my key."

He'd sent back the key for the garden gate, along with an extravagant bouquet of yellow hothouse roses. Red ones would have been a little too obvious. "I respected your decision."

"Yet here you are."

"Would you like to come driving? I picked up a flashy new pair of horses at Tattersall's this week, and I think you'll like putting them through their paces."

Lady Verena Gerard was a better driver than most men in the ton. When Eliot saw the grays, he'd known straightaway that they'd take her fancy.

As he drank in the details of her appearance, he frowned. When she'd turned up, he'd just been so bloody grateful that she hadn't tossed him out on his ear. He'd paid no attention to what she was wearing. "In fact, I see that you're already dressed and ready."

Her scarlet carriage dress looked spectacular. The severe cut and the military frogging made him more aware than ever that he and Verena fought a battle. It also made the blood rush hot in his veins. Fine wool material clung to every luscious inch of the body that he hadn't enjoyed in the last fortnight. While his heart might yearn for her, his need was achingly carnal, too.

A huff of unamused laughter escaped her. "You've caught me in an inconvenient moment, my lord."

He hid a wince. They'd been on first-name terms since that first glorious coming together in a cold and blustery Leicestershire. "I can come back later, if you like."

"I wish you wouldn't." She sent him a straight look. "The affair is over. You even said as much, the last time we spoke."

Interesting that she recalled his words. Did that mean she, too, had stewed over that fraught encounter at the Lumsden ball? Or was Eliot clutching at the frailest of straws?

"Yes, I did say that, didn't I?"

When he stepped closer, her eyes widened in alarm, before she straightened her shoulders and stared him down. He was painfully aware that she hadn't invited him into a private room. Hell, she hadn't even asked him to sit down. He felt like an importunate tradesman chasing up an unpaid bill.

"Then why visit me?"

He shot her a direct look. "The affair is over, Verena." He watched relief fill her features, and almost hated knowing how short-lived it would be. "Because the courtship has begun."

"Don't be a fool, Eliot." She went white again, and this time she retreated. "You've got too much to lose."

He found it in him to smile. "And even more to gain."

A bitter smile twisted her lush mouth. "You're mad to say that. Once everyone is gossiping about you, and you're a laughingstock in society, and your political dreams have turned to rubble, you'll come to your senses. But it will be too late to repair the damage. Then, if you're like every other man I know, no doubt you'll blame me."

His laugh was wry. "My sex hasn't done much to impress you, have we?"

Her smile, such as it was, faded. "If you proceed with this absurd pursuit, you'll inconvenience me, you'll embarrass yourself, and you'll spoil Imogen's season. Whatever we shared is over. So far, you've escaped from my clutches without causing a scandal. Say a grateful prayer for your luck and move on."

Stubbornness spiked, while agonizing hurt tangled his gut into knots. "I'll never move on from you, Verena."

"Then you're inviting a world of pain and humiliation. How can I say this more clearly? There's nothing further between us."

She sounded so sure. Damn it, had he given her his heart with no hope of her returning his feelings? He refused to believe it.

Yet she sounded so adamant when she denied him. Was that because of what her bastard of a husband had done to her? Eliot would wager half his fortune that when they'd been lovers, she'd felt more than mere desire. He also suspected that she couldn't turn off that feeling simply because she wished she could. That must be only one of the many things that terrified her.

"Do you truly feel nothing for me?" He wondered what he'd do if she said yes.

What he'd do if she said yes and he believed her.

For a brief moment, those beautiful blue eyes revealed a distress to match his own. But before his hopes could revive, she controlled her expression. "Until you started this nonsense, I felt kindly toward you. I enjoyed our time together, and it was fun to know that the most respectable man in London was being very wild indeed in my bed. Neither of those things mean that I looked forward to a lifetime in your company."

"Is that the best you can do?" Eliot asked, hating her dismissive tone.

"I wish you well in the future."

"Don't you dare say that we can be friends," he said in a taut voice.

She shrugged. "Hardly. We move in such different circles, after all."

"If you're going driving, why not come driving with me?"

"You know why. It's the same reason why when you visited me, you sneaked in via the mews instead of through the front door." Verena frowned. "Did you say you arrived in a carriage?"

He smiled. "It's outside."

"On the street?"

"Yes."

A furrow appeared between her fine eyebrows. "How can you be so impulsive? There's no point to this. If you know anything about my affairs, you must have heard that I never take a man back, once I've had my fill of him. Your behavior will only spark the scandal that you've worked so hard to avoid."

Eliot didn't flinch, although every time she told him that it was over, it stung like the blazes. By heaven, he should go. No gentleman forced himself into company where he wasn't wanted.

But some deep instinct kept shrieking that he wasn't alone in still feeling the powerful attraction that had brought them together. Did Verena love him? Buggered if he knew. The odds weren't good. But he was sure that she wanted him. Just as he wanted her.

"Then what harm to come driving? If you care so little for me, why should you worry if people say I'm just one more gentleman who has fallen under your spell? We both know it's true."

At his ardent declaration, her eyes rounded and he caught a glimpse of the warm, passionate creature who filled his dreams. "Eliot—"

A sharp knock on the door made her blink and turn away. "I'm engaged to drive with someone else this afternoon." Then with a sudden burst of genuine feeling, "Plague take you, why don't you go when I tell you to?"

His gaze didn't waver. "You know why."

He knew that she wanted to berate him for his persistence, but she fell silent when Merton arrived to let in the mysterious visitor. It would be a man, Eliot knew.

Was it the scoundrel who would replace him in Verena's bed? He knew that she still wanted him, but he also knew that she was running scared. At this moment, she was het up enough to run straight into another man's arms.

"Please get the door, Merton," she said clearly. "Lord Colville is just leaving."

"Very good, my lady," Merton said. It had always amused Eliot that the boldest woman in

London employed the capital's starchiest butler. He wasn't amused today.

Merton opened the door, and Eliot found himself trapped in a nightmare.

"Good afternoon, Verena. What lucky sod owns that dashing rig outside? Those nags are two of the prettiest horses I've seen in a dog's age."

"Good afternoon, Shelburn," Verena said with a calmness that contrasted with her earlier crossness. She looked pleased to see the bastard, curse her. The bastard looked pleased to see her, too, as if someone proffered a delicious morsel to tempt his jaded appetite.

It was clear now who was taking her driving. It was clear for whom she'd put on that far too becoming red ensemble. Very deliberately, Eliot uncurled his hands from the fists that they'd formed when Shelburn appeared. He resented the man's presence. Even more, he resented the way that the villain seemed to be at home in this house.

Eliot hadn't expected such an eligible rival. Leighton Anstey was far too handsome, and a dashing rake besides. That was something that nobody had ever called Eliot.

Had Verena decided that Shelburn was her next lover? Before she took up with Eliot, she'd demonstrated a penchant for picturesque rogues, and Shelburn certainly fit that description. The man was well known for his taste for lovely women. Eliot couldn't even deride him as a brainless flibbertigibbet. The toad was more than just an impressive physical specimen. He had a good mind, too.

Just the sort of man Verena would find appealing.

Eliot had long ago noticed that she sought Shelburn's company. They were regular dance partners. Were they about to become partners in sin as well?

Not if he had anything to say about it, by God.

"Lord Colville called unexpectedly." Verena's tone was light, as if seven months of secrecy didn't shatter around them at this very moment.

"Good afternoon, Shelburn," Eliot said with impressive coolness, given how much he wanted to knock the reprobate onto his arse. Despite the surface politeness, the air bristled with masculine aggression. "I dropped by on the off chance that Lady Verena might favor me with her company in the park."

Eliot's presence provoked derisive amusement in Shelburn. Probably because his lordship couldn't imagine what a dull dog like Lord Colville would want with the wayward widow. Or more likely that he pictured how the wayward widow would snicker to learn that a paragon like Eliot Ridley harbored an interest in her.

"I never thought to see you here, Colville." Shelburn regarded Eliot with an assessing stare that he couldn't like. "Shouldn't you be out, performing good deeds for the greater benefit of the masses or something?"

The smug swine. How Eliot burned to wipe that superior smile off the man's highbred face. But if he did, he might as well push Verena straight into the blackguard's arms. She wouldn't appreciate the sight of two of her suitors brawling in her front hall, and she'd blame Eliot for any fracas.

Eliot bared his teeth in a savage smile. "This afternoon, the masses will have to manage without my assistance."

"I see," Shelburn said, when it was clear that he didn't see at all, although he'd dearly like to.

"But as you and I already have an appointment, Lord Colville is just on his way," Verena said.

Even the world's most insensitive man would know that he wasn't welcome. Eliot ignored a lifetime of training in manners and stayed to study Verena and Shelburn, trying to work out how far their flirtation had progressed.

He hadn't heard anything about Shelburn and Verena linking up. And unlike his affair with her, there was no reason to hide a liaison with the libertine earl. But then, it was only ten days since she'd sent Eliot away. Perhaps she and Shelburn were sorting out the details.

However much he wished it wasn't the case, he couldn't help admitting that they looked perfect together. Verena's lush beauty and Shelburn's lazy charm made them a striking couple. The earl was a swarthy fellow with a touch of the gypsy about him. Black hair. Black eyes. Black eyes all for Verena at the moment, blast him. The impulse to punch the rapscallion surged higher. "I thought the lady might like to try my new carriage horses."

"They were giving your tiger a bit of trouble outside when I came in. He was trying to walk them, and they were showing every sign of wanting to bolt."

Damn it all to hell. Eliot needed to take over from Tom before the grays caused an accident. He'd arrived optimistic enough to hope that he'd call for Verena, and they'd be on their way. Instead, he'd lingered to plead his case, and she was going off with Shelburn anyway.

"They're a fiery duo, that's for sure."

Shelburn's glance indicated that while the horses might be fiery, he feared their owner wasn't. "They need a good driver."

Eliot bit back a growl at the implication that they needed a driver other than him. Arrogant brute. "I'm up to them," he said with a mildness that he didn't feel.

"I'm sure," Shelburn said with a conviction that he clearly didn't feel either. He turned to Verena, who had remained uncharacteristically quiet through this exchange. "Shall we go, my lady?"

She turned to Shelburn with a brilliant smile that Eliot knew was for his benefit. Perhaps she imagined that if he believed she'd already taken a new lover, he'd leave her alone.

Would he? The longer he was with Verena and Shelburn, the less he was convinced that she was on fire for the earl. Hard as she worked to give Eliot that impression.

For a start, he knew what Verena looked like when she craved a man. He sensed a fondness for Shelburn, who was an old friend, but nothing more. The crackle in the air was missing.

The air had crackled when he arrived this afternoon, no matter how she'd tried to send him away. That crackle had always been so obvious to him that he wondered why nobody else had ever picked up on their flaring attraction.

Call Eliot a naïve fool, but he didn't think her quite lost to him yet.

"It's a lovely afternoon," she said and held her hand out to Shelburn, who took it and tucked it into his crooked elbow.

Shelburn's glance was supercilious. Could he make it any more obvious that he didn't rate Eliot as a rival? "Good luck with those horses, Colville. I look forward to seeing you put them through their paces in the park."

He looked forward to Eliot making a complete cake of himself, rather, was the barely hidden message in the patronizing comment.

Eliot shortened the rein on his temper and bowed. "My lord. My lady." He shot Verena a sharp look. "Perhaps another time I'll find you at leisure, Lady Verena."

"Perhaps," she said with more of that infernal coolness that made him want to seize her and kiss the haughtiness from those full, red lips. See how high and mighty Shelburn felt then.

Eliot followed the couple outside. As he put on his hat – Merton hadn't even taken his hat and topcoat, a signal that a long visit wasn't encouraged – he saw that Tom was indeed struggling to restrain the grays.

The door shut behind him while Eliot lingered on the top step. He watched Shelburn hand Verena into a high-perch phaeton, drawn by two chestnuts much more disciplined than his cattle. Although right now, they caught the grays' nerviness and sidled with unease in a footman's hold.

As Verena took her seat, she hardly cast a glance at Eliot's rig. Shelburn climbed up beside her and raised his whip with a flourish that Eliot felt was unnecessary. But then the villain had always been more flash than substance. A quality that never seemed to hamper his success with the ladies.

"Hold on, Tom. I'm here," he called to the boy and ran down the stairs to leap into his curricle and take up the reins. Subject to a firm hand and the voice of authority, the horses soon settled.

"I'm sorry, my lord, but the nags wouldn't pay no heed to me, once Lord Shelburn's carriage arrived."

"Never mind." Eliot smiled at the lad who had come up from Gloucestershire with him. Tom Ball belonged to a large family that had served the Ridleys for generations. "I shouldn't have left you alone with them so long."

Tom looked relieved that he wasn't about to cop a scolding. Shelburn's carriage rolled past with Verena looking sternly ahead. In a strange way, Eliot found that reassuring. If he truly meant nothing to her, she wouldn't try so hard to give him the heave-ho.

To his surprise, Shelburn touched the handle of his whip to his stylish beaver hat. "Well done, Colville. Your cattle looked ready to make a break."

Eliot gritted his teeth, although he heard genuine admiration in the words, instead of the usual mocking insolence. He bowed with his own hint of insolence, then turned to his tiger. "Jump on, Tom. We're off to the park to give these two beauties a run."

With a cheeky grin, Tom obeyed. Eliot had hoped to leave Tom at Verena's house, while he stole the chance for a private conversation. That wasn't to be, sod it. But be damned if he was going to come out with his new pair, just to turn around and go home with his tail tucked between his legs.

He wanted to prove to Verena that he no longer cared if scandal attached to his name. No time like the present to launch his campaign.

CHAPTER SEVEN

"That puffed-up buffoon handles the ribbons better than I thought he would," Shelburn said. "Maybe those magnificent horses aren't wasted on him after all. I feared he'd ruin them with plowman's hands."

"What did you say?" Verena was paying no attention whatsoever to her escort. Instead, she felt as though she contained a stormy ocean inside her. She hadn't been alone with Eliot since he'd proposed in that horrid scene at the Lumsden ball. He still had the power to turn her world upside down.

She'd spent the last ten days, telling herself that she'd soon forget him. Ten awful days while her body hungered for his touch and she'd hardly slept. It was almost worse when she did sleep, because phantom memories of Eliot's lovemaking tormented her dreams.

She'd decided that the best way to get over him was to avoid his company, which given that high society was one large village was more difficult than she'd prefer. And while she'd maneuvered not to dance with him or fall into conversation with him, the effort involved hadn't done much to help her forget him. Nor had seeing that golden head across a crowded room night after night. She strove not to notice him, but striving was another thing that kept him uppermost in her thoughts. Every direction she looked, she was in trouble.

Even worse, he seemed to turn up at every event that she attended. What on earth was Eliot up to? If he continued his pursuit, the talk would soon be all over Town. People might even wonder if something was going on between Lord Colville and Lady Verena.

Fate had an ironic sense of humor. When she and Eliot had been mad for each other and conducting a clandestine affair, nobody in society had suspected a thing. Now that they were no longer involved, Eliot's wayward behavior was sure to attract unwelcome attention. When wayward was a word that she'd never thought to apply to the viscount.

As if to underline his resolve to play a part in her life, the elegant yellow curricle passed them at a fast clip. Eliot looked uncharacteristically rakish with his visible ease with the reins and his high-crowned hat at an angle. She had to agree with him about one thing. She'd very much like the chance to test her skill at handling those grays. They were such sweet high steppers, they made Shelburn's elegant chestnuts look like cart horses.

"Colville turns out to be quite the whip. Who would have thought the prig had it in him?"

Verena bit back the urge to stand up for Eliot. It was harder than it should have been. "It appears he has hidden talents," she responded in what she prayed was a noncommittal tone.

The problem with Shelburn was that he'd known her since she was toddling. He'd been her first dance partner at Claremont Castle, the ancestral home of the Dukes of Horsham where she'd grown up. If she wasn't careful, he was apt to see past her pretense of indifference to the handsome viscount.

"Indeed." Shelburn stopped speaking to negotiate his way around a mail coach. By now, Eliot was a hundred yards ahead, weaving through the thick traffic with a deftness that she couldn't help but admire. "In fact, it turns out that the saintly viscount is a man full of surprises. Including his presence at your house when I called this afternoon."

"It doesn't mean anything." This was just what she feared. Curiosity was inevitable, and it made her want to box Eliot's ears. "I'm not at all his sort of woman."

When Shelburn studied her face, she prayed that she didn't look as shifty as she felt. "I wouldn't have said so, but perhaps I'm wrong."

"Are you saying I'm unfit to associate with him?" she snapped, tightening her grip on the rail along the edge of the seat.

He cast her another curious glance. "Not at all."

"But you suspect he thinks that I'm unfit to associate with him."

"It's clear that he doesn't think that, if he called to invite you driving. In fact, I'm wondering if the fellow has his eye on you. It's not the first time that he's singled you out. He danced with you at the Lumsden ball, before you two went off alone together."

She shrugged, inwardly appalled at how closely Shelburn had been observing her. "We took the air. There's no sin in that, is there?"

"Except it was as cold as a witch's tit that night. Nobody was out on the terrace or escaping into the garden in search of privacy. And when I found you in the hallway, you were looking rather peaky. Did Lord Incorruptible make his move, Verena?"

Damn Shelburn and his sharp eyes and even sharper brain. Damn Eliot for ambushing her with his proposal at a ball, instead of somewhere private where she could hide her agitation from society's busy tongues.

"You seem to be paying a little too much attention to what I do and who I do it with," she said in a tight voice.

Despite his low laugh, his eyes remained watchful. "I have a brotherly interest, given that your actual brothers have washed their hands of you, the mealymouthed hypocrites. Hillary does nothing but chase opera dancers, while Eustace has a string of bastards from the mistress he's kept all these years. And that's as well as fathering six children on that poor downtrodden wife of his."

"I don't need looking after," Verena said through stiff lips.

"You know, I'm not sure that's true." He paused as if waiting for an objection, but she didn't respond.

To her relief, he went back to concentrating on his driving. The chestnuts were biddable beasts, or at least they were in Shelburn's skilled hands. But the street was crowded with vehicles and pedestrians. Eliot's skill in negotiating the throng while in charge of those frisky horses was doubly impressive. Because they'd never appeared together in public, Verena hadn't realized that he was a first-class driver.

Once he'd cleared the snarl of carriages at Hyde Park Corner, Shelburn returned to the topic of Viscount Colville. To her annoyance. "Although the last man I'd ever expected to have to save you from is that epitome of rectitude, Eliot Ridley. You will tell me if he becomes a pest, won't you?"

"You're making too much of this," Verena said.

"Am I?" Shelburn said in a musing tone without looking at her. "I'm not sure. There was a look in the paragon's eyes that tells me he has plans for you. And when I teased him, he looked ready to murder me."

Once again, she wanted to leap to Eliot's defense when Shelburn belittled him. She needed to abandon her allegiance to her former lover. After all, Eliot Ridley now meant nothing to her. "That's just because you were being impossible."

"Perhaps. And perhaps the viscount suffered an attack of the green-eyed monster when he learned you were driving out with me and not with him."

Eliot, Eliot, Eliot, what have you done?

It was becoming harder and harder to maintain her disinterested air. "You're basing an awful lot of speculation on one dance a couple of weeks ago and an invitation to drive in the park, especially when his lordship took his dismissal in his stride."

Which was a lie, but Shelburn didn't need to know that.

Shelburn shook his head, keeping his attention on his horses. "Except that small amount is more than I ever imagined he'd do. He's always so all-fired determined to keep a lilywhite reputation. Showing you any attention at all screams louder than another man taking off his clothes and dancing around naked in front of you."

Verena forced a laugh and hoped it sounded more natural in Shelburn's ears than it did in hers. "Goodness, I hope that's not how my next lover intends to woo me."

Shelburn didn't laugh. "Speaking of lovers, you haven't taken one in a donkey's age. Are you reforming, Verena? Or has something been going on that you haven't told your dear old chum Shelburn about?"

Oh, no. Verena's heart plummeted into her stomach. If Shelburn started thinking too hard about all this, he'd winkle out every one of her secrets before they reached the park. "I vow, Shelburn, you make me sound like Messalina. I don't have a new man in my bed every night. In fact, I sleep alone more often than not." Always, in fact.

Shelburn's expression grew serious as it rarely was. "I imagine after being married to George Gerard, that's a relief."

It was, but it wasn't something that she wanted to talk about now. Or ever.

She'd done her best to hide the scars that her marriage had left behind. The thought of the world feeling sorry for her made her skin creep. But to her regret, Shelburn knew her too well to fall for the carefree widow act. "I choose my lovers. I lay down the rules they follow."

Except for Eliot. Oh, he'd cooperated with any request that she made, but from the first, he hadn't fitted the pattern of her other paramours. That exceptional status continued. At the end of an affair, no other lover had left her unsettled and unhappy and second-guessing herself the way that he did.

Right now, she wished to the devil that she'd never met him.

"I think that's one of the reasons why you infuriate so many men. You act like they do."

She shrugged. "Few women have my freedom."

His next words dashed any hopes of moving on from the subject of her bed's recent occupants. Or the lack of them. "But even when you're between lovers, you're on the hunt. I haven't heard your name linked with any gentleman's, since you sent Oscar Peary on his way and he fled to France to nurse his broken heart."

"It wasn't that bad."

"Believe me, it was. The fellow looked ready to throw himself into the Thames, the last time I saw him."

Oscar had been a nice man and an enthusiastic lover. A little too enthusiastic. When she'd noticed signs that their association was becoming more than an amusing diversion for him, she'd ended it.

Why in heaven's name hadn't she seen that things tended the same way with Eliot? If she'd sent him off after a few delightful weeks, she wouldn't be in this mess.

Now she paid the price for being greedy for more pleasure, more...Eliot.

"I'm sure Oscar's having a perfectly enjoyable time in Paris and he's forgotten me altogether." She paused. "And saying I'm on the hunt doesn't present a very flattering picture."

Shelburn frowned at the horses. "It's more flattering than you imagine. I always think of you as Diana the huntress."

She responded with a derisive snort. "Diana was a virgin goddess."

When he glanced at her, Shelburn still looked serious. "I know it sounds mad, but no matter what happens to you, no matter what you do, something about you remains pure and untouched."

The thought was so absurd that she broke into a peal of laughter. Quite natural this time. Once she'd caught her breath, she curled her fingers around Shelburn's elbow. "In that case, six months without a lover should suit me down to the ground."

He still didn't smile, and the look he sent her banished any further desire to laugh. "If you say so, Verena."

By the time they joined the crowd flooding into Hyde Park for the fashionable hour, Shelburn had recovered from his uncharacteristic urge to delve into the secret corners of her soul. Verena discovered that Eliot's new team of horses and stylish carriage were subject to much admiring comment. The people she met were agog at this new dashing version of proper Viscount Colville.

Everything in the world seemed to conspire to keep her focused on the scoundrel.

Except if she was honest with herself – and she usually was – she thought of him every five minutes anyway.

She told herself not to look at him, but couldn't help herself. He'd stopped to talk to the Tierneys and then the Bilsons, who were strolling through the park with Imogen. The girl looked spectacular in a dark blue walking dress with black velvet braiding.

"She's a fine-looking chit," Shelburn said, noticing the direction of Verena's attention as Eliot took Imogen up beside him. "The *on dit* is that Halston plans to offer for her before the season is out."

Shocked, Verena turned to him. Eliot had mentioned that bombastic oaf Chippenham as a potential suitor. The dissolute Lord Halston was an altogether different proposition. "Really? I hadn't heard."

"He invited her down to his place in the country last week."

"Just her?" If he did, it was as good as a proposal.

Shelburn gave a wry laugh. "No, you silly girl. There were plenty of other people there, but her father is boasting all over London that his daughter is about to become the next Countess of Halston.

Halston has singled her out, and he usually shows no interest in debutantes. Haven't you noticed how often they dance together and how he's started attending the sort of respectable ton events that he once wouldn't touch with a bargepole?"

Verena regretted to say that for the last ten days, she'd noticed very little apart from how miserable she was and who Eliot chose to dance with. "She'll make a pretty bride," she said, as she struggled to match the dissipated earl with the innocent girl.

It seemed absurd, but she felt very protective toward Imogen. Perhaps because she saw something of herself in the spirited girl with an ambitious and tyrannical father.

"She will. And she's rich besides, not that Halston needs the blunt."

Eliot had turned his rig in their direction and with a sick feeling, Verena realized that he headed toward them. The cautious man that she'd first known would never think to introduce his sister to his mistress – or former mistress. But this new, unpredictable Eliot was likely to do anything.

"Good   God,"   Shelburn   said,   genuine amazement sharpening his voice from its usual lazy drawl. "Colville is coming this way."

Verena sat up straight in the seat and shot Eliot a blistering glare from under the brim of her stylish peaked hat. He ignored her displeasure, and his daredevil smile showed no trace of fading as he pulled in beside Shelburn's carriage with a neatness that in other circumstances Verena might commend.

Verena knew that she wasn't alone in observing the viscount's approach. While she maintained the cool control that had served her so well since discovering the unpleasant reality of life with George Gerard, her skin prickled as hundreds of well-bred eyes settled on the little drama playing out under the trees.

Plague take Eliot, what he did would only fan gossip about his intentions toward Verena. Respectable intentions at that. He may as well shout another proposal from Mayfair's rooftops.

Part of her – the untamed, reckless, selfish part – almost admired his effrontery. His daring as a lover had taken her by surprise and enchanted her too fast for her to raise her usual defenses. But throughout their affair, he'd played the sensible, practical fellow in public. This unfamiliar, dangerous version of Eliot thrilled her to the bone.

But that didn't mean that she approved of him throwing away his future by making this overt claim on her. He was in the grip of spring fever, but when he recovered his senses, he'd kick himself for this outlandish behavior. Especially as he'd find himself without either sterling reputation or lady. She'd sworn that she'd never marry again, and she meant it.

"Lady Verena. Lord Shelburn," Eliot said, sweeping his hat from his head with a grace that sent a ripple of unwilling awareness down Verena's spine. "The park is busy this afternoon. The fine weather must have brought everyone out to enjoy the sun."

Highly likely. So far, it had been a dank, cold spring.

"No doubt," Shelburn said. To Verena's regret, his eyes gleamed with more of that pestilential curiosity that she'd tried so hard to quash.

"Lady Verena, may I present my sister, Lady Imogen Ridley, who is enjoying her first season in London?"

What could she say? "I'd be delighted to make her acquaintance."

"Imogen, this is Lady Verena Gerard, who is one of society's brightest ornaments."

Imogen looked surprised at that description. So was Verena. Eliot was known as a plain speaker. She just had to recall that desperate, roughly expressed proposal to remember that. Although she never liked to recall his proposal. The memory always made her stomach clench in anguish.

"Good afternoon, Lady Imogen," Verena said with a smile. "I hope you're enjoying your time in Town."

Up close, the girl was exquisite. Shining raven hair, neat features, white skin and large blue eyes alight with intelligence. Verena wasn't surprised to hear that Lady Imogen had ensnared one of the ton's most elusive catches. She'd make a spectacular countess.

"Good afternoon, Lady Verena. Good afternoon, Lord Shelburn." Imogen responded with a politeness that in no way reflected the searching stare she leveled on Verena. "Thank you for asking, my lady. It's all been so exciting. Not at all like Gloucestershire."

"I'm sure," Verena said, liking that Imogen made no pretense to a sophistication that she was too young to own. "I hear you've just come back from Buckinghamshire."

"That was exciting, too. Lord Halston was a wonderful host, and Prestwick Place is quite magnificent. Do you know it?"

Verena examined the girl's face for some sign of smugness because she'd captured the rake, but all she saw was open enthusiasm. No blushes. No bashful fluttering of the eyelashes.

Interesting. Could it be that the rake was beguiled, but the innocent wasn't? If Halston proposed and Imogen refused him, that would put the cat among the pigeons.

Then she recalled Lord Deerforth, and a sick feeling settled in her midriff. She hadn't wanted to marry George, but a parent was in a position to compel consent.

"Yes, I've been there several times. The grounds are glorious."

Eagerness lit Imogen's eyes, and Verena recalled Eliot saying that his sister had an interest in garden design.

Eliot had observed Verena's proper interactions with his sister with an approval that in no way made her forget that he was being very improper indeed. Verena Gerard wasn't a suitable companion for a fresh-faced girl just out of the schoolroom. They both knew that.

Now his laugh was almost a groan. "Don't mention the grounds, my lady. Imogen has been waxing lyrical about terracing and water features since she came back to Town yesterday. If she gets started now, we'll be here until next week."

Imogen cast her brother a teasing looked that combined censure and fondness. Verena couldn't help approving of the unconcealed affection between the two siblings. She'd always suspected Eliot was a good brother. Now she knew he was.

Or he had been, until his headlong descent into scandal.

"I'm sure you exaggerate," Verena said.

Imogen rolled her eyes. The gesture was charming in its naturalness. In general, debutantes were rather a dull lot, too conscious of making a good impression. But Imogen sparkled. The match with Lord Halston seemed more feasible with every minute.

"I'm sure he doesn't, my lady," Imogen said.

Shelburn laughed. "Talking about gardens would make a nice change. The last debutante I danced with entertained me with a long discussion about lace on bonnets."

"I hope we can discuss Prestwick Place on some other occasion. I see Lady Edgecombe over there, and I have something particular to say to her." Verena slid her fingers around Shelburn's arm in a deliberate gesture that she meant Eliot to notice.

While he appeared relaxed, she sensed his alertness. He bristled like a guard dog ready to snarl at the slightest provocation. She supposed he was seeking some sign that he returned to favor. That telltale muscle flickered in his cheek, and the grays shifted in harness, as if the pressure changed on the reins.

Eliot bowed. "I'll see you tonight at the Pollock ball. Perhaps you'll keep me a waltz."

Shelburn's arm twitched under Verena's hand, as she struggled to summon an answer to his effrontery. "I'm sorry. I'm otherwise engaged this evening, my lord," she said, silently cursing him. He must know that he created trouble with no hope of reward.

It seemed that a night at home loomed ahead. At least it meant that she wouldn't be on edge about Eliot's next move.

"What a pity," he said easily, while his eyes told her that none of this was easy at all. "Some other time?"

"Perhaps," she said through tight lips. "A pleasure to see you, Lady Imogen. Shelburn, we should go. Lady Edgecombe never stops long in the park." Plump Celia Edgecombe would rather recline on a well-padded sofa with a box of bonbons and the latest Minerva Press novel than do anything that smacked of exercise.

After polite farewells, Eliot urged the grays to a trot and his carriage rolled away. Verena sucked in her first full breath in twenty minutes, forgetting for a moment that Shelburn sat close enough to notice her response. She waited for some pointed comment on that meeting with Eliot and her reaction to it. But he remained silent as he turned his attention to his horses.

That was the most worrying thing of all.

CHAPTER EIGHT

As was inevitable, Eliot's father ordered him into his presence three days later. He was surprised that the earl had taken so long to react. He'd expected a report of his encounter with Verena in the park to reach his parent's ear within the hour. The Pater was getting slow in his old age.

Eliot strolled through a beautiful spring afternoon to Lorimer Square, where his father had rented an opulent house for Imogen's season. The weight in his gut was familiar from childhood, although at least today his father was unlikely to beat him for his sins, the way he had when Eliot was a boy. It always struck him as odd that while he'd long ago lost any respect for his father and thanks to a godmother's generosity, he no longer relied on the old man for money, the words, "Your father wishes to see you," still turned his blood to ice.

Brent the butler opened the door and took his hat. "You've got his lordship in a right spin, Mr. Eliot. Everyone downstairs has been walking on eggshells the last day or so. He knocked one of the maids down this morning, because she made too much noise putting fresh eggs on the breakfast table."

Brent and he were old friends. As a child at Hamble Park, Eliot had often run to the servants for comfort after his father's temper had left him bruised and bewildered, and wondering why he always did something wrong when he tried so hard to do right. While it might be many years since Brent and his wife, the housekeeper, had mopped up blood and tears after an encounter with his enraged sire, the fondness remained.

"Send the girl to Trentham Hall, if she wants to leave my father's employ. I'm sure Mrs. Oates can find a place for her." A fair proportion of the staff at his country estate were refugees from his father's violence.

"Thank you. She's a good lass." He and Brent shared a steady look that spoke of years of cleaning up the results of his father's anger. Several times, Eliot had asked Brent to work for him in Wiltshire, but the man came from a long line who had served the Earls of Deerforth. And as he said, he needed a more challenging role than running a house that Eliot seldom visited. Challenging certainly described Lord Deerforth's household.

"Is he in the library?"

"Yes."

"And where are Imogen and Stella?"

"Lady Imogen and Miss Stella are paying calls this afternoon, I believe."

"Let's hope that he's cooled down by the time they come back," Eliot said without much optimism.

Over recent years, his father's resentment of Eliot's growing independence had only deepened. Their rare encounters grew ever more acrimonious. Today's promised to raise the roof, so he was glad that his sister and his cousin were out of the house.

"Indeed, Mr. Eliot," Brent said, and Eliot's heart sank further as he heard an equal lack of conviction in Brent's voice.

"Don't show me through. I can make my own way to him." He'd make his own way in any case, but that didn't mean he looked forward to the histrionics to come.

While he'd kept his rooms at the Albany during his family's stay in London – he only lived under his father's roof when he couldn't avoid it – he knew his way around the house from his visits to Imogen. The library was on the ground floor at the back, overlooking the generous garden. All these houses on Lorimer Square occupied what were, in London terms, large plots of land.

He walked along the corridor and knocked on the closed door at the end.

"Come," his father barked from inside.

With grim fatalism, Eliot opened the door and stepped into the library. "Good afternoon, Father."

With difficulty, Lord Deerforth rose from behind the large desk and glared at his only son. As a younger man, he'd been handsome, but years of bad temper and self-indulgence had taken their toll. There was a portrait of a young Deerforth at Hamble Park that could have been a picture of Eliot. But little of that angelic, golden-haired gentleman remained now.

The earl was still tall, but time had added stones to his weight and the chiseled features had coarsened and settled into a permanent peevishness. He looked what he was – a selfish brute with no tolerance for anything but his own desires and opinions.

Eliot couldn't remember ever loving his father, but as an adult, he'd come to hate him. If he hadn't been so fond of Imogen and if he hadn't owed a duty to the family name, he'd have broken off relations long ago.

"Well may you call me father when I'm ashamed to call you son."

Eliot bit back a sigh. He already saw that this was going to turn out to be one of his father's more self-righteous tirades. "I'm sorry to hear that," he said with the deliberate calmness that he always cultivated with his sire. It drove Deerforth demented when his temper raised no reaction. Eliot had started it to annoy his father, but these days, he was calm because mostly he just didn't care.

"Sorry? Sorry? *Sorry*?" Deerforth repeated on a rising note. "You should be on your knees and begging my pardon, you brainless fool."

Eliot arched his eyebrows and spoke even more coolly. "Is that so?"

His father hadn't invited him to sit down. These days, Eliot didn't seem to be a welcome visitor wherever he went.

"Don't pretend that you don't know why I called you here." His father lumbered out from behind the desk. His bulk and height always conveyed a threatening air, although Eliot was now two inches taller and his days of cowering beneath his father's overpowering anger were long past. "Not even you could be as stupid as that."

Eliot's supposed lack of intelligence was an old insult, and one that had long ago lost its sting. He rested his weight on one hip and folded his arms with an appearance of casual interest. "I assume you've heard of my pursuit of Lady Verena Gerard."

His father growled and stepped close enough to breathe into Eliot's face. This time, only the strongest willpower kept Eliot where he was. The reek of stale tobacco smoke and brandy would topple a weaker man. "You dare to speak that whore's name in this house?"

Eliot met his father's glittering eyes. His voice emerged edged with icicles. "You will not insult the lady in my presence, sir."

His father snarled. "She's no lady. Her name is infamous throughout the land. And you had the temerity – the madness – to introduce this harlot to your innocent sister? What the devil were you thinking, you idiot? When I heard the tale, I didn't believe it. By God, you've always been a disappointment, but that you should show such profligate disregard for the most basic rules of propriety leaves me speechless."

Unfortunately that was far from the truth. If only it was. "Lady Verena is a duke's daughter, and she's accepted everywhere. I'm proud to call her my friend."

His father went an alarming shade of crimson and puffed up with such fury that Eliot feared for the old boy's health. "Proud? The woman is a living example of vice and degradation. You will wait in this house and apologize to Imogen for exposing her to such contagion. Then you will break off all connection with this shameless harpy."

Eliot found it in him to smile. It was either that or punch his father in the jaw. "I'm afraid that's impossible, sir. I intend to make Lady Verena my wife."

His father's color flared even higher, and he staggered back to seize the mantelpiece in a shaking hand. "You..."

For once, Eliot had succeeded in silencing his father, but there was no satisfaction in it. The earl looked like he was about to suffer an apoplexy.

Eliot filled a glass from the decanter of brandy on the desk and extended it toward the gasping man. "Father, drink this."

"Sod off, you swine," the earl said with an uncontrolled gesture that caught Eliot's hand. The glass flew out of his hold and shattered on the fireplace surrounds. "I don't need your pity. I'm all right. Or I would be, if I had a son who hadn't lost his mind. What the devil insanity is this? If you want the wench, go ahead and fuck her. A thousand other men have."

Eliot's eyes narrowed on this ranting hypocrite, familiar to every brothelkeeper in London. "If you were one ounce fitter, I'd beat you to a pulp," he said through lips that felt like they were made of wood. "As it is, I bid you good afternoon. I'll inform you when I've gained Lady Verena's consent."

His father gulped in a mouthful of air and straightened, although his hand still gripped the edge of the mantel so hard that the knuckles shone white in his fat fingers. "So you haven't asked her yet?"

Eliot paused in the act of walking out and faced his father. "Yes, I have."

Then he wished to blazes that he hadn't admitted that. It gave his father the advantage.

"But she hasn't given you an answer." His father studied him with the contempt that he was used to. "Wait, she did answer. But she said no, didn't she?"

The problem with his father – one of the many problems with his father – was that while he might be a loathsome individual, he possessed a razor-sharp mind. What Eliot would give right now to present his marriage to Verena as a fait accompli. "I hope to persuade her of the advantages of the match."

Deerforth broke into a delighted cackle and started to look a little better to Eliot's relief. "Bugger me if I don't almost admire the wench. She knows she's no fit wife for you. She knows she's no fit match for any man. At least old Horsham taught her that much, and she's no fool, even if she's got the morals of an alley cat. I wish my son had half her brains."

"As I said, I've proposed and I intend to press my suit," Eliot said in a flat voice, one hand closing into a fist at his side. How he itched to smash that crowing leer from his father's face. Maybe if the man was ten years younger and ten stone lighter, he might have done it.

"She won't say yes. Whatever else she is, she's a woman who knows what society will accept."

"I believe you're wrong."

His father must have felt on firmer ground because he took an unsteady step toward Eliot. He made a visible effort to sound calmer. At last, he gestured Eliot toward a chair. An invitation he ignored.

"Come, lad. Put this insanity behind you. If you persist in associating with this woman, you'll lose any chance of making your mark in parliament. They're talking of you as a future prime minister. You've got a brilliant career ahead. You can place your stamp on the country. Don't you want that? Don't you want to make your old dad proud?"

What Eliot wanted was a chance to shove his old dad's teeth down his throat. He reminded himself again that he, more than anyone, knew violence solved nothing. Enjoyable as clouting the earl might prove.

"No, I don't." He didn't point out that his father wasn't talking about him as too stupid for his own good anymore. His father had never been one to let logic lose him an argument. "The only thing I want is to be Lady Verena Gerard's husband. That would indeed be an achievement worth boasting about."

His father jerked as if Eliot had struck him, and the temper stirred again. "Then to hell with you. I can't stop you. You're of age, more's the pity. It makes me sick to the stomach that I can't bar you from the succession. You're not fit to hold the Deerforth title."

Eliot's disdainful bow conveyed no respect. "You're entitled to your opinion."

"I won't inform Imogen of your blatant disregard for her welfare and reputation. It will only cause her distress." If his father loved anyone, he loved Imogen. And she'd always had the knack of handling the old man better than Eliot ever did. "I'd like to avoid a scandal as long as I can, although if you continue along this absurd path, you'll ruin the whole family in the end, you useless cur."

In truth, Eliot felt a twinge of guilt about the impact that his courtship might have on Imogen's season. Although as he'd said to Verena, the girl was such a catch, her brother's behavior wouldn't destroy her long-term prospects. "If I wed Lady Verena, Imogen will know."

"I hope she's safe by then. The engagement to Lord Halston is close to done and dusted. I'm expecting him to offer for her any day now."

"Yes?" Eliot asked, not liking where this was going. He hadn't been paying as much attention as he should to Imogen's beaux. The end of his love affair with Verena had left him too sunk in despair.

He'd heard rumors about his sister and Halston. The man struck him as too experienced for a girl of only twenty. His reputation as a ladies' man wasn't much better than Shelburn's. On the other hand, Eliot could imagine that the licentious earl was more to Imogen's taste than prosy, middle-aged

Lord Chippenham. And perhaps Halston was sincerely in love with Imogen. Eliot might be biased, but he thought that his sister was a genuine prize. Too good for Halston, in truth.

Of course, whispers of engagements were meat and potatoes to society. Most of them ended up being as insubstantial as sea mist. But Halston had danced with Imogen at every ball that Eliot had attended lately. Not to mention that the man had invited Imogen down to the country for his recent house party, which seemed a marked sign of favor.

"I can't stop you from pursuing this disastrous course, much as I want to," his father said. "But if you have an ounce of love for me, if you have an ounce of love for your sister, don't do anything to spoil her chances with Halston. Her marriage to him will be a triumph, and it will put her out of reach of the catastrophe that you threaten to bring down on this family."

Eliot frowned. His father sounded desperate, which wasn't his usual manner. His standard tone was command, not entreaty. Despite everything that had just passed between them, Eliot couldn't help considering his father's request. Because while he didn't give a rat's arse about his sire, he dearly loved his sister.

If Imogen wanted Halston and he wanted her, Eliot owed it to her not to stand in their way. He pointed out the obvious flaw in his father's plan. "The season has just started. What if Halston doesn't propose until August?"

What if Halston didn't propose at all?

"Then give me a month." Pity made an uncomfortable bedfellow with Eliot's long-standing hatred. "Why the devil would Halston delay, if he's found the girl for him? And he must know Imogen doesn't lack for admirers. He won't want to take the chance of losing her."

Eliot's lips closed against an instinctive urge to deny his father. Verena wouldn't wait a month to choose another lover. That oily bastard Shelburn was already hanging about like a bad smell. Every time Eliot turned around, the rogue was dogging Verena's steps.

On the other hand, Eliot continued to pursue Verena because he suspected that he was more to her than just a passing amusement. If she forgot him so easily, perhaps he should just accept his broken heart and give her up.

Not to mention that he owed Imogen his loyalty. He'd never underestimated the almighty scandal that would break out if he and Verena married. Their association would set every tongue in society wagging, which was one of the reasons that he'd tried so hard to keep their affair secret until now.

He was willing to pay the price to win the woman he loved. But must his sister pay the price, too?

"A month's delay won't change my mind about marrying Verena," he said coldly.

Eliot knew his father well enough to realize that he didn't just make this plea on behalf of Imogen's happiness. The earl hoped that if his son had time to weigh consequences, he'd repent of his imprudent intentions. But none of that changed the fact that wooing Verena could disadvantage Imogen.

"That may be," the earl said. "But it will give Imogen a chance to marry the man she wants. When Halston proposes, she can push for a quick wedding. I doubt he'll kick up a fuss."

The man she wanted, not to mention the man with the Prince Regent's ear and a network of connections at the top levels of society and business. His father wasn't thinking of Imogen's heart, but how he could take advantage of his influential son-in-law.

"After a month, you will make no public complaint about my courtship of Verena. If we marry, you'll come to the wedding."

Displeasure flashed in the earl's eyes, but after a moment, he nodded. "Agreed."

Eliot despised his father, but the stamp of parental approval on the match might start to rehabilitate Verena as a respectable member of society. Given Imogen's situation, what else could Eliot do but cooperate?

Squaring his shoulders, he told himself that it was only four little weeks. He tried not to think of how this last fortnight since his beloved had broken with him had seemed to last a thousand years. He could survive a month. Even if Verena took another lover, it didn't herald the end of his hopes. Although every masculine cell in his body howled in protest at the thought of her turning to another man.

Taking a deep breath, he bent his head in grudging surrender. His heart remained heavy. "In that case, we have a deal. I'll delay my wooing of Lady Verena for a month, or until Halston and Imogen sort everything out between them."

His father's gloating smile deepened his disquiet. He didn't trust the earl not to do his best to use these four weeks to scupper Eliot's hopes.

CHAPTER NINE

While he mightn't trust his father to keep his promise, Eliot was a man of his word. For the next week, he retired to his estate in Wiltshire. If he said that he'd stay away from Verena until Imogen and Halston's engagement became official, he would. Which consigned him to a run of sleepless nights, while his imagination ran amok, picturing her with another man in her bed. Usually that scoundrel Shelburn.

Even worse, none of his copious correspondence was the chatty, gossiping kind. While every day, he received a pile of letters detailing parliamentary business, he didn't hear a whisper about whether Lady Verena Gerard had taken a new lover.

Eventually, the agony of not knowing outweighed the agony of being in Verena's presence, but unable to claim her. He returned to Town.

He called on Imogen, who as yet wasn't betrothed to Lord Halston. For once, he managed to talk to her alone without Stella being there. Stella was out of sorts and had retired to her room with a headache. Even better, his overbearing father was out. Deerforth always dominated the conversation.

To Eliot's surprise, when he asked about Halston, Imogen didn't react like a girl in love. Instead, she responded with some amusing tales about the house party and how much she'd enjoyed it. In fact, she waxed much more lyrical about the grounds of Prestwick Place than she did about its owner. Then she and Eliot went on to speak of other things.

If an engagement was likely before the month was up, he saw no sign of it. Imogen was her usual self. Bright. Funny. Sweet. Could it be that the interest was all on Halston's side?

Puzzled, he left his sister and prepared to join some friends at the opera. But the caterwauling singers and the illogical plot couldn't hold his attention.

Even then, he still had no idea whether Verena had moved onto a new paramour. Eliot's usual crowd were much readier to talk party politics than society tattle about who was sleeping with whom. If he hadn't promised his father to keep his interest in Verena out of public view, he might have asked.

After the first interval, he left the theater, blue-deviled and restless. Eliot hoped to hell that Halston and Imogen soon made their connection official, or he'd be a complete wreck.

His rooms were only a short walk away. Perhaps some fresh air would settle him enough to sleep. Not that he'd wager a groat on that happening. Since his debacle of a proposal, sleep had become a stranger.

He had a grim feeling that he'd spend tonight the way that he'd spent every night over the past three weeks. Staring into a glass filled with brandy that he had no real interest in drinking.

After Verena had refused him, he'd tried seeking oblivion in alcohol, but neither his liver nor his generally sober tastes allowed him any solace. In fact, the idea of sinking into more lonely self-pity was so unappealing right now that he walked past the Albany and up toward Green Park. He didn't want to admit it, but he was heading for Verena's house in Half Moon Street.

Not that mooching about on the street would offer relief for either his curiosity or his longing. She wouldn't let him in, even if she was home, which at ten o'clock on a Wednesday night at the height of the season wasn't likely.

Sick of himself, sick of the world, sick of being without the one woman who made sense of his life, he was wandering along Piccadilly with the dark expanse of the park on one side when a carriage pulled up beside him. Without turning to look, he hoped to Hades that it wasn't someone wanting a conversation. Pretending he hadn't noticed, he started to walk a little faster.

The carriage rolled forward, and he heard a door click open behind him. Damn it, he'd have to summon up some manners, when all he wanted was the chance to be alone to nurse his heartache.

No, that wasn't quite accurate, and he was a man with a reputation for sticking to the truth, however unpalatable. All he wanted was Verena back. To his eternal regret, that wasn't likely to happen any time soon.

The urge to disappear into the shadows was almost overwhelming, but for twenty-nine years, he'd been trained to be a gentleman. So he stopped and turned around and struggled to assume an expression of polite interest. He didn't expect trouble. The carriage was expensive and drawn by the sort of blood stock that the average street thug didn't aspire to own.

"Eliot?"

His irritation vanished as if it had never been. His knees turned to water, and the breath jammed in his throat. On unsteady legs, he took a step forward to where the door stood open in welcome. Dear God above, let it be in welcome.

"Verena?" He leaned in to peer inside. She didn't have the lamps on inside the vehicle, so the interior was dim. But the lights on the exterior lent enough illumination for him to catch the gleam of her eyes and the glitter of diamonds at her throat and dangling from her earlobes. "What on earth are you doing here?"

Her gesture was visible through the gloom, thanks to her long white satin glove. To his surprise, the movement conveyed a weariness that mirrored his own. "I live around the corner."

As if he'd forgotten that. He even smiled with no hint of sourness, when he couldn't remember the last time that he'd done such a thing. "I know, but it's so early."

At least in society terms. Most balls didn't start until ten and went through until several hours after midnight. People who dedicated themselves to the season turned into nocturnal creatures.

"I went to the Plunket ball, but it was all just the same people doing the same thing, so I decided to come home. What about you?"

More surprise flooded him, not least because this was the friendliest that she'd sounded since she'd finished with him. But also because Lady Verena Gerard was an essential component of London's dazzling social whirl. Since her husband's death, she'd seized every opportunity for entertainment. She was more likely to be dancing until dawn than traveling home alone, just as the beau monde stepped out on display.

Alone? Did that mean anything?

Unfortunately he doubted it. Lady Verena might take a lover if she fancied him, but she slept by herself. Eliot had never spent the night at her house.

He summoned up an answer to her question. Anything to keep her here. "I was at the opera."

"You didn't enjoy it?"

"No." He hadn't enjoyed much at all since they'd parted. "Horrid load of drivel."

"You sound rather down in the dumps."

"So do you." Which was odd, because even when Verena wasn't herself, she always did her best to hide it. He imagined that she'd learned to hide a lot of things during her marriage to that brute George Gerard.

A silence fell, broken only when her horses whickered and shifted, making the harness jingle. The coachman said a quiet word to calm them. It reminded Eliot that he should let her go, even if she didn't seem in any hurry to move on.

"Your horses won't like standing," he said, not wanting her to leave, but not sure how to detain her. His skin ached with the need to touch her. All the warmth in the world lived with Verena. Since he'd been without her, his days had been so cold.

He waited for her to close the door and order her driver to proceed. But she made no move to finish their meeting. "I haven't seen you lately."

Surprise turned to astonishment. Could she have missed him? "I've been down at Trentham Hall."

"The country must be lovely right now."

The wistful note in her voice left him even more confused. Verena's marriage settlement had granted her a small estate in Devon, which she never visited, as far as Eliot knew. She was made for urban delights.

"Yes, it is," he said, although if he admitted the truth, he'd hardly noticed the glories of spring. He'd been focused on an inner landscape that encompassed nothing but beige.

"Get in," she murmured, which struck him as the most astounding thing that she'd said yet.

He straightened. "The Albany is out of your way."

Her low laugh was a bitter reminder of how easy they'd once been with each other. "I'm going home."

Discontentment gnawed at him. Why the devil couldn't they be together now? They'd been so perfect.

"I know you were on…" He hesitated, in part because his heart slammed against his ribs so hard that it stole his ability to speak. Did she – could she – be saying what he thought she did?

Surely not. For weeks, she'd avoided him. But if she relented, be damned if he'd miss out because of pride or a lack of nerve.

Nonetheless, the risk of asking, only to receive another rebuff turned his voice toneless as he phrased the question. Because he had to be prepared to hear her say no. When it came to handling her, he'd already been wrong so many times. "Are you asking me to come back to your house with you, Verena?"

He felt her studying him from inside the carriage. "Would you like to?"

He'd sell his soul for the chance. But he wanted to make sure that he understood. "Yes, I would. Do you wish to talk to me?"

"I imagine there might be some talking involved."

"And other things?" For days, heavy chains had encased his heart. Now his heart broke free and started to race with an excitement that contained a powerful dose of hope.

"Get in the carriage, Eliot. You know you want to." Her voice held an irritable fondness that sounded sweeter than any of the yowling singers that he'd heard at tonight's opera. "For pity's sake, what are you waiting for, you great dunderhead?"

By God, he was a dunderhead. He'd wanted to see Verena, and here she was. Even better, just at this moment, she didn't seem to hate him.

He climbed inside and shut the door behind him, as he sat down opposite her. She rapped on the roof, and the carriage lurched into movement.

"I thought you never wanted to see me again," he said somberly, wishing there was enough light to read her expression.

"I didn't." She snatched a shaky breath. "But mad as it is, I've missed you. I've even missed you dogging my footsteps and scowling at me whenever I smile at another man."

"I don't like you smiling at other men, when you have no smiles for me."

"I feared you might have forgotten me when you no longer appeared at my elbow every time I turned around."

"Forget you?" His laugh was hollow. "I'll be a dead man before that happens. Even then, I suspect I'll come back to haunt you."

It was true, but he didn't go on to mention how much he loved her. He didn't want to risk her tossing him out on the cobbles, at least not until he'd had a chance to remind her how good they were together.

Eliot waited for her to dismiss his answer, but she remained silent. He didn't speak again either, partly because there was too much to say and they were only yards from her house. Partly because of late, everything that he said to her just seemed to drive her further away.

He intended to tread with care to make sure that he didn't bugger things up. Fate had provided him with a miracle. Verena was here. Tonight, he'd take her in his arms again.

Anticipation spiced his blood. She'd invited him back to her bed. Surely he hadn't got that wrong. He'd missed everything about Verena, her touch, her scent, the sound of her voice, the way the world only felt the right way up when he was with her.

But while he made a pretense of being a civilized man, it wasn't the entire truth. He'd also missed thrusting into that glorious body and feeling her clench tight around him when she reached her peak. He loved her soul, but he loved the earthy reality of her, too.

With a bit of luck, a dose of earthy reality awaited tonight. God – or the devil – be praised.

The carriage rolled to a smooth stop in front of Verena's tall white house. Eliot was accustomed to sneaking in through the garden when he visited for sinful purposes. Entering the building through the front door held an intriguing touch of the forbidden.

A footman ran down to open the carriage door and hand Verena to the pavement. Eliot climbed out after her, his heart racing with excitement and a powerful dose of gratitude. He hadn't been sure that he'd ever find a welcome in this house again. Now he was here at Verena's invitation and looking forward to taking her to bed.

He didn't touch her. The desire sizzling between them meant he wanted privacy before he laid a hand upon her. Because he feared that when he did, he'd go up in flames and he wouldn't come down again before they'd both burned to smoldering ash.

She climbed the steps to the open door. Light flooded from the hall to illuminate her in gold. She was gold to Eliot. She always had been.

Turning on the top step, she smiled at him the way she used to, as if he was the special lover, the one who could take her to heaven and back. "Eliot, are you coming in?"

He realized that he lingered below her, lost in a dream of what he meant to do to her. Whereas tonight against all expectations, he didn't have to dream. Luscious reality beckoned.

A self-derisive laugh escaped. "Thank you."

He wasn't just thanking her for inviting him into the house.

As the carriage trundled away behind him, Eliot mounted the steps two at a time. At last, he took her arm, sliding his hand under the folds of her heavy blue velvet cloak to find the bare skin above her satin glove. Even through his kidskin glove, the immediate heat of contact rushed through him, made his heart stop for a moment. No other woman had ever wielded this power over him.

Verena gave a start, as his fingers encircled her upper arm. Her breath emerged in an audible hiss. She felt it, too. The hunger. The need. The longing.

It was the same as it had been at the beginning. Better. Now he knew what profound pleasure this invincible physical link promised to deliver.

Eliot released Verena so Merton could take the cape. Beneath the luxurious midnight blue folds, she wore an azure gauze gown decorated with gold lace. The effect was like sunrise after night.

Or perhaps that was just how Eliot felt about the world right now.

"That's a dashed becoming frock," he said. "I haven't seen it before."

"Thank you." As a widow, Lady Verena had become a leader of fashion. During her marriage, George had kept her wrapped in drab colours and high necklines that threatened to strangle her. "I was moping around last week and hoped a couple of new dresses might cheer me up."

"Did they?"

The look that she shot him struck hot as a bolt of lightning. "What do you think?"

"I think that a beautiful girl shouldn't be unhappy."

Her red lips curved upward in a smile remarkable for its sexual promise. "I'm not unhappy now."

"Nor am I."

She *had* missed him, by Jove. If Merton hadn't been waiting beside them in his usual dour silence, Eliot would have dragged Verena into his arms and kissed her until she couldn't see straight.

"My lord?" Merton said in his sober fashion, although he must sense that he stood in the middle of a storm of unspoken desire. "May I take your hat?"

Without shifting his gaze from Verena, Eliot handed over his hat, coat, and stick. The action reminded him of his last visit, when he hadn't managed to get beyond the hall.

He waited for Verena to head into the drawing room, offer him a brandy, perhaps explain this extraordinary change. But she cast him an incendiary glance under her thick dark brown eyelashes, and made straight for the staircase.

Eliot had never used this staircase before either. When he was a regular visitor, he'd come to his mistress via the backstairs. Her staff must have been aware that he was in the house. Luckily, Lady

Verena Gerard had the most discreet servants in England.

Did this mean that Verena was at last ready to acknowledge him as her lover in public? Even as a prospective husband? It wasn't as if his interest in her was a secret from the ton any longer.

His heart drumming, Eliot followed Verena up the spectacular curved staircase. His gaze fixed on the saucy sway of her hips under those elegant blue skirts, while expectation beat a fierce rhythm inside him. Merton had left the hall, but still Eliot didn't touch her.

She turned down the corridor leading to her bedroom. This was more familiar territory. Pacing along the carpet after Verena, he couldn't help but recall every other time that he'd walked this hallway and the revelations that he'd discovered at the end.

Outside the closed door, she glanced back with another of those irresistible come-hither looks that shuddered through him like a blow. "Eliot—"

But he'd reached the limits of his patience. Damn it, the limits of control.

A single stride brought him up to her. He lashed his arms around her and swept her up for a kiss that told her how lonely he'd been without her, how elated he was to be with her now.

CHAPTER TEN

*V*erena released a breath that veered toward a sob and surrendered to the fierce demand of Eliot's lips. Her hands rose to plunge into thick golden hair and bring his mouth harder against hers.

How she'd missed this. Without Eliot's passion, life became a barren wilderness.

Since she'd sent him away, she'd put on a brave face. Even tried lying to herself, which never worked. But with the first touch of those deft hands, all her pathetic self-deception disintegrated. She didn't want to need this man. She didn't want to need anyone. But Eliot Ridley was as necessary to her happiness as air was to her life.

She'd resented his pursuit of her – largely because she had to make such an almighty effort to resist the temptation of giving him everything he wanted. But then a little over a week ago, he'd stopped appearing at society events. She'd wondered with an unpleasant shock whether at last he'd accepted his dismissal.

A huge ragged wound had split her guarded heart. She hadn't realized quite how wretched she'd feel when there was no prospect of seeing Eliot or talking to Eliot or even being in the same room.

She'd had a rotten week of no sleep, amid the usual frenetic activity that lately gave her no pleasure. When had her wild whirl of gaiety stopped being compensation for everything that George had once denied her? When had it instead become an unsatisfying gyration just to stay in one place?

All the time that she'd danced and flirted and gossiped, she'd yearned to see the man she'd rejected. It made no sense. She and Eliot were too different to be together. But without him, she felt aimless and lonely and on edge.

So now she teased him with her tongue, to show him how she'd starved for him. She crushed her body into his, as if she tried to crawl inside him. She drew his rich masculine scent deep into her lungs.

He slammed her hard against the wall beside the door, making the picture near her head rattle in its frame. Through the tornado of kissing, she felt him release the front fall of his trousers. When his penis sprang forward to press into her belly, a shiver of uncontrollable excitement crashed through her.

Verena loved it when he was tender. That always made her feel cherished and special, like the innocent girl she'd once been, before her life took a very dark turn indeed.

But she also loved it when desire turned him savage and uncontrolled. Eliot was so desperate for her now that she could smell it on his skin. Heat all but steamed off him.

With shaking hands, she reached down to shape that hard column of flesh rising between his legs. All that magnificence would soon stretch her deep inside. She couldn't wait. Insistent throbbing set up in all her secret places, so violent that it verged on pain.

When Verena squeezed him, he groaned against her mouth and nipped at her lips. The sting stoked the fire of her arousal. In wordless encouragement, she moved her hand up and down his cock.

He caught her under the hips and hoisted her high against the wall. With an incoherent growl of approval, she hooked one hand around his neck and wriggled in his hold. She wanted to put her legs around him, but this fashion for straighter skirts was a cursed nuisance.

Verena shifted again, and this time his groan held real agony. His dick surged in the most delicious fashion against her stroking fingers.

"If you keep doing that, I'll come in your hand," he grated out, his voice harsh with lust.

How she'd missed his unabashed craving. Eliot was the most alluring mixture of outward restraint and inner explosiveness. Some nights, when she glimpsed him across a crowded ballroom, the knowledge of the volcano of passion lurking under that perfect exterior turned her insides liquid. Because that volcano was all hers, part of the secret Eliot who was Verena's alone.

"It's this pestilential skirt," she muttered, in between peppering his face with frantic kisses. "I want to put my legs around you, but I'm all tangled up."

"Hold on."

He shoved his hips forward, cramming her against the wall. Supporting her with one hand under the rump, he shoved up her skirts to reveal fine white stockings above dark blue satin dancing slippers tied at the ankles. He slid her skirts higher, uncovering filmy white petticoats and the lacy edges of her drawers.

"Tear the blasted rag," she said in a choked voice, as she leaned back, gasping.

His laugh was a mere grunt. "It's too pretty to ruin."

"I don't care about it." She felt like she dissolved into a pool of hot honey. "I must have you."

If he didn't take her soon, she swore that she'd explode from sheer frustration. She'd wanted him and missed him for weeks, but she'd forgotten quite how inflammatory his touch was. The slightest brush of his hand always threatened to set her alight. Just now, he promised to do much more than use his hands on her, thank God.

He shifted, and for a moment she feared that he might lose his grip on her. Instead, he fumbled with the froth of skirts and petticoats, until her legs were free to curl around him. She exhaled with relief and angled forward to rub her cleft against that impressive cock.

It wasn't enough to take the edge off her appetite. She needed him inside her.

"Well done, Eliot," she said in a choked voice.

This time his laugh was recognizable as such. "That sounds like you're congratulating me on a good cricket stroke."

Her laugh was a breathless huff. "With luck, you'll do a lot of stroking."

"Later," he said on a long exhalation. "Now I've got to have you or die."

"Yes, later," she said, grabbing his neckcloth.

It took her longer than it should, but she managed to undo the knot and fling the length of linen away. She buried her face in the warm hollow of his throat and breathed deep of his humid male scent, spiced with arousal. Better than roses. Better than baking bread. Better than fresh coffee. This was the scent of home and pleasure and Eliot. The scent of heaven. The best smell in the world.

When she kissed the notch in his collarbone, his pulse pounded beneath her lips. The knowledge that his very blood clamored for her made her smile with appreciation. When she'd feared that he no longer wanted her, the world had turned dark and cold. She'd felt empty without him, and she'd hated it.

He bumped forward, until at last he pressed just where she wanted him. A flood of warmth greeted him and soaked her frail cambric drawers. When she raised her head to kiss him again, she met a ferocious welcome that had her writhing.

Her movements set up a pleasing friction, but it still wasn't enough. Her legs bent more sharply to widen the angle of her thighs. When one knee struck something, a loud crash penetrated the thunder in her ears.

The sound made her glance to the side. A large Chinese vase, one of a series lining this corridor, lay shattered across the parquetry floor. The one on the opposite wall had lost its twin.

Eliot's laugh was as breathless as hers. "Oops."

She didn't give a toss. "Take me, Eliot," she gasped out. "I need you."

He adjusted his hold, fumbling as her weight slipped and almost dropping her. A shocked cry escaped her, and she tightened her grip on his shoulders. This was a bumpy ride, and all the more thrilling for the occasional awkwardness. Eliot was usually a graceful, skillful lover. This clumsiness told her that he'd missed her as much as she'd missed him.

One hand dug hard into her hip, as he cupped her mound through her drawers. She shuddered as another wave of arousal hit her.

By the time Eliot found the slit in her drawers, every brush of his fingers against her intimate curls and sensitive lower belly had her jerking in his arms. Her sex quivered and spasmed in longing. Already she verged close to climax. Her breath emerged in erratic bursts, while he was panting as if he'd run all the way from Wiltshire.

When he found the place that sent sensation blasting through her, Verena whimpered. Material twisted tight around her, followed by a ripping sound as her drawers shredded. Before she'd completed her gasp of surprise, he pushed inside with ruthless intent. Every muscle in her body clenched in shocked pleasure, and she ignited into rapture before he started to move.

Since he'd kissed her, she'd felt on the brink of orgasm. His body uniting with hers flung her over the edge. Heat coiled in fiery spirals, set her shaking in uncontrollable response, quaking and crying out in wonder.

She dived into the inferno. Towering response lifted her high, until she was dizzy and helpless. After poising on those giddy heights for an untold span, she crashed down to drown in a seething ocean of rapture.

It felt like an age later that she drifted away from that searing release. As the real world gradually resumed its place in her mind, she gulped air into starved lungs. She was staring at a painting of York Minster hanging opposite her, and Eliot's tall, strong body jammed her against the wall in the hallway.

In the hallway!

She was lucky Merton hadn't come along to check the house for the night. Dear Lord above, he'd have got the shock of his life if he had.

In most cases, Verena had enough self-control to make it into the privacy of her bedroom before she pounced on a lover and demanded satisfaction. Even with Eliot, whose briefest glance could send her up in smoke.

Tonight, she'd been so famished for his touch that she'd lost all connection with where she was. Eliot was lucky that he'd got as far as the first floor before she flung herself at him.

He'd buried his face in the curve of her neck. His breath was moist against her bare shoulder. Somewhere in that furious mating, one sleeve had slipped down her arm.

He breathed so hard that each exhalation emerged as a soft groan. His cock fit snugly inside her, filling every longing inch. He remained hard and ready. She'd succumbed to that earthshaking climax without him having to do much to arouse her.

When they'd first come together seven months ago, she'd been sure that such white-hot need couldn't last past the initial intoxication. Desire never had with her other lovers. Yet with Eliot, every sexual encounter was richer and better and more blazing. It didn't matter whether he took her fast or slow, her body melted into helpless surrender every time.

"God above, I've been so lonely for you, Verena," he muttered, his voice muffled against her skin. His lips moved in a phantom kiss on the sensitive nerve running down her neck to her shoulder.

"Oh, Eliot…" she sighed, wanting to tell him how she'd missed him, too. But before she could speak, the muscles of his back flexed under her palms, and he began to move.

She shuddered under every purposeful plunge, feeling him penetrate deep. The sensation was so satisfying, even though she knew that with each thrust, he claimed more of her than just her body.

Before she could worry about that, another climax hit, short, sharp, blinding. York Minster dissolved into a mist of broken colours, while rapture flooded her and blasted her thoughts to powder.

Verena was panting with blazing pleasure when she felt him stagger. For a fraught second, his hands dug into her hips, then he wrenched free, breaking the hold of her legs around him. As her legs unfolded beneath her, she was grateful for the wall behind her. She still shivered with the last vestiges of ecstasy, and she wasn't sure that she could stand on her own.

He lurched back, releasing her and wrapping one shaking hand around his penis. With a guttural groan, he lost himself in his fist. The skin clung to the bones of his face, and his jaw was sharp and hard as flint as he pumped into his hand. His golden skin was flushed, and his eyes were jammed shut.

Still struggling to drag enough air into her lungs, Verena slumped against the wall and watched him with a hunger that she couldn't hide. Since exiling him from her bed, she'd struggled to pretend indifference. What a waste of time. After what they'd just done, only a fool would think that she didn't ache for him. And Eliot was no fool.

"That was marvelous, Eliot," she forced out of a tight throat.

Slowly he opened eyes that were dark and heavy as they leveled on her. "It's only ever like that with you," he said in a gruff voice, as he fumbled for his handkerchief and cleaned himself off.

"It's the same for me." That sizzling encounter left her too overcome to summon her usual self-protective irony. What was the use? Her responses betrayed her craving. No amount of smart talking would convince Eliot that she didn't care.

He pocketed his creased handkerchief and tucked himself back into decency, although she could have told him that there was no point. She meant to have him naked again, the moment that she got him on the other side of this door. They had a lot of time to make up for.

"Come into my room." She reached for his hand. "I believe you offered to stroke me."

How had she managed without him these last few weeks? The stark truth was that she hadn't managed.

When he surveyed her from head to toe, his eyes lit with the laughter that always made her feel like the world was a better place. "I can't believe that I've just been through the most debauched encounter of my life, yet you're still fully dressed."

Verena cast a rueful glance down at the torn drawers, sagging around her ankles. She supposed she should be grateful that her stylish new dress had survived. "Almost."

She stepped out of her drawers and bent to pick them up. As she rose, dazed eyes took in the utter devastation surrounding them. Shards of expensive porcelain scattered everywhere. She hadn't shattered alone, it turned out.

When Eliot noticed the direction of her gaze, a wry smile curved his mouth. "Sorry about the Ming vase."

She stifled horrified laughter. "Merton will have a fit. He loves my china more than he loves his wife, I vow."

Eliot laughed, too, as he reached up to straighten the picture beside her head. Then he drew her close enough for a gentle kiss. His tenderness brought tears to her eyes, so when she pulled away and stared at him, candlelight formed a halo around his golden head. The awful truth was that while she might once have mocked him as a saint, now she knew how fine he really was.

Verena was sickly aware that she was nowhere near good enough for him.

CHAPTER ELEVEN

*E*liot stirred and tightened his arms around a sleepy, naked Verena. He was pleasantly tired and physically satisfied, and at ease with the world in a way that he hadn't been since she'd broken with him. Since before that. He'd long ago grown discontented with the small part of herself that Verena was willing to share. But in asking for more, he'd ended up with nothing at all. How desolate that had left him.

He had no idea what time it was. Somewhere in the early hours. The fire had burned down, and the candles guttered in puddles of wax.

Verena had never before let him stay the night. He liked sleeping with her. He liked it very much indeed.

When they'd retired to her room, they'd taken their time making love. She'd asked him to stroke her and he'd obliged with relish, lingering over her breasts and giving her another climax with his mouth on her quim. Then he'd spent what felt like half an eternity in heaven, rocking against her slowly until they both reached a peak of such rapturous delight that he felt made anew.

Now she lay with her back pressed against him, her silky hair drifting over them. He nuzzled it out of the way so he could drop a kiss on her bare shoulder, while his hand shifted to cup one full breast. He closed his eyes to sleep again, but she made a drowsy murmur and slid closer.

"I went to sleep," she murmured. "I didn't mean to."

"So did I," he said, cuddling her closer. Their Friday afternoons had been glorious, but short and packed with sensual adventure. He certainly wasn't complaining about that, but there was such sweet contentment in holding the woman he loved in his arms on a cold night and knowing that he didn't need to be anywhere else.

"I haven't been sleeping since you went away," she said with a yawn.

Since she'd given him orders to go, rather than since he went away, but he was too in charity with the world right now to argue the point. "Me either."

She shifted in his arms, turning to kiss him. He tasted longing on her lips and something that might be love.

Verena drew away and studied him through the dimness. Her fingers trailed over his face, tracing the lines of cheekbones and nose and jaw, as if she learned him by touch alone. He closed his eyes and made a sound that was close to a purr.

"I'm so glad you came back, Eliot."

His blood warmed under her searching hand. "So am I."

"I hoped you'd come to your senses. We already have so much. Why spoil it with asking for the impossible? Will you come to me again on Friday?"

His lazy enjoyment slammed to an abrupt end, as his awakening mind made reluctant sense of what she was saying. The tragedy was that she sounded so happy, as she ground his heart to dust beneath her delicate heel.

Eliot went rigid and jerked back from her caressing hand. "I'm not going back to what we had, Verena," he said, his voice still weighted with sleep.

He was foolish enough to pray that he'd mistaken what she said. The thorny silence that descended told him that he hoped in vain.

She wriggled out of his arms and pushed up against the pillows until she rose above him. "But you came with me when I invited you tonight."

A sour grunt of laughter greeted that remark. "Of course I bloody well did. I've been a wreck without you. Having you back has been like rain in the desert."

"Then be my lover again, Eliot," she said, and he knew she frowned at him through the darkness. "I want you. You want me. We're wretched when we're apart."

A great weight of grim misery rolled over him. More painful than ever, now that he'd had this reminder of what bliss he found with Verena. These last hours had been among the most spectacular of his life. Yet right now, he wished that she'd driven right past him near Green Park.

He climbed out of the bed and lit a taper from the fire. Without looking at Verena, he prowled around the room lighting fresh candles. Just now, he couldn't bear the sight of her. She was too beautiful and too dear. And his heart was too close to breaking for him to cope with either of those things.

"Eliot?" she asked after a few moments, when she hadn't received any response. "What do you say? Don't be so stubborn, my darling. You know you're far from ready to finish with me. Why, you went off like a rocket tonight. One touch, and you were mad for me."

His lips tightened, as he stared into the fire, keeping his back to her. He'd said that he had no pride when it came to Verena, but it seemed that he wasn't yet ready to show her quite how devastated he was right now. "I'm always mad for you. I've been mad for you from the first word you spoke to me."

"Then don't let pride take you away. I'm mad for you, too."

Her declaration didn't ease his unhappiness. He started to gather his clothes, which took longer than it should. He'd flung his garments everywhere, once he made it into the privacy of her bedroom. From the hallway where he'd taken her up against the wall, where any of the servants could have walked past and caught them.

Mad for her, indeed.

"Aren't you going to answer me?" Verena said, more in puzzlement than anger, as she watched him head toward the dressing room.

"Not while I'm buck naked," he said with a calmness that he didn't feel.

She glared at him, although he caught a glimpse of the familiar fear. How odd to realize now that he'd always thought her the bravest woman he knew, yet the tragic truth was that she was crippled by terror. Perhaps the fact that she lived with that terror, yet defied it with every breath, constituted her true bravery.

"In that case, let yourself out from the dressing room and go home." She was trying to sound like the woman who had sent him away at the Lumsden ball. She wasn't succeeding. "We have nothing more to say to each other."

He gave her a sad smile. "We've got a lifetime of things to say to each other, if only you'd realize it, Verena. But I'll start with tonight."

She was back to looking sulky, and she'd pulled the covers up to her chin, as if they defended her against him. "You're just going to ask me to marry you again."

"Probably."

"And I'll just say no again."

"That's your right."

"So you may as well go."

As he trudged through to the dressing room, he didn't answer. He had things to say, but he felt too vulnerable putting his heart on the line yet again, when he stood in front of Verena without a stitch to cover him. Already he felt as if his longing heart beat on the outside of his body, providing a clear target for Verena's arrows.

She'd still most likely strike him down, but at least his black evening wear would hide the blood.

Verena stayed where she was and waited to hear the door close from the dressing room to the outer corridor. Her heart was heavy, even as her body glowed with physical pleasure. But then, Eliot's skill as a lover had never been in doubt. It was everything else that was the problem. Everything else made her so angry that she'd happily smash another Chinese vase over his head. And keep on smashing, until the house was devoid of expensive porcelain, and he saw sense.

It had been a mistake to stop and take him up in her carriage. It had been even more of a mistake to invite him in. After that, the mistakes had piled one on top of the other so fast. Now they towered so high that they threatened to collapse and crush her.

But she'd been so downhearted and sunk in a mire of longing when she saw the familiar silhouette walking along Piccadilly in the dark. It had seemed like fate offered her another chance with Eliot.

It turned out that fate was a nasty bitch.

What fate offered was a reminder of the magic he could make with her body – as if she needed that, after weeks of sexual frustration! Then a final ending to their affair.

Because it seemed that he hadn't given up his lunatic notion to marry her, while she only wanted to go back to having him as her lover. There would be no compromise. She'd seen his face when he left the room. Never in her life had she seen a man look so determined.

Well, she was determined, too.

Not that she took any joy from it.

After this, she could never invite him back into her bed, which meant no more Eliot for her. Not just no more of those adept hands and his powerful possession. But no more talking to Eliot, or laughing with Eliot, or finding in Eliot's kindness a safe refuge from an often cruel world.

It was enough to make a girl want to throw a tantrum and hurl things and curse the path her life had taken.

Why, oh, why had her perfect lover decided to change things? Plague take Eliot, the gallant, muddleheaded beefwit. She should have known from the first that he'd cause her trouble.

Verena was in such a lather of temper and regret that when she heard the snick of a latch, she didn't immediately realize that it was the door to her room. She was so worked up that she felt like she'd swallowed a hive full of angry bees, buzzing to be free and stinging her over and over.

How mortifying that Eliot should catch her with tears pouring down her face. When George died, she'd vowed that she'd never again cry over a man. To hell with Eliot Ridley, he turned her into a liar as well as a soggy mess.

"Oh, Verena..." he said with such remorse in his voice that she couldn't bite back a shuddering sob. Remorse and love, although she didn't want to hear the fondness underlining the dismay. "It's not the end of the world."

Her hands clenched in the blankets, as she drew them higher. An absurd action, as there wasn't an inch of her naked form that Eliot hadn't explored to their mutual enjoyment. "Yes, it is."

Through bleary eyes, she watched his smile turn tender. Which didn't do much to stop her bawling. Having a lover who wanted her was nothing new. But only Eliot ever looked at her as if he lived to cherish her. She'd miss that, too, devil take him.

Why did he have to adopt this stupid stance? Why couldn't he be what she wanted him to be?

Except so often before, other people had put her on the receiving end of that wish. Starting with her overbearing prig of a father. He'd wanted a quiet, obedient, proper daughter, and he'd done his best to achieve that with his fists and other punishments. He'd never defeated her spirit. Nor had George, who had used similar methods of coercion.

She'd never bowed to him either, not in her heart. Knowing that he'd failed to subdue his wife had tormented him to the day he died.

If she had a right to choose what she wanted, so did Eliot. She just wished that he wanted what she did. Futile as that wish was.

He glanced around. "Where do you keep your handkerchiefs?"

"In the top of the chest of drawers," she said in a choked voice, wiping her eyes with the crumpled sheet. The smell of their bodies on the linen only reminded her of their untrammeled pleasure, and how she'd felt whole in his arms tonight in a way that she hadn't since he'd gone away.

"I'd lend you mine, but it's not clean," he said, crossing to open the drawer and pull out a flimsy square of lawn and lace.

Nonplussed, he frowned at the handkerchief. She couldn't blame him. His handkerchief was large and practical and made to handle a crying fit like hers. That drift of frail white that looked so ludicrous in Eliot's elegant masculine hand was purely for show.

He put it back and closed the drawer. He collected a towel from the top of the chest and crossed to pass it to her. "This might be more up to the job."

"I must look dreadful," she said, then cursed how vain she sounded. But she'd never been a pretty crier. Her nose went red, and her eyes swelled up, and she made horrid gasping sounds, as if she drowned in quicksand.

He responded with a wry affection that had her snuffling through another rush of tears. "You've looked better, I must admit."

Her raspy laugh surprised her. She felt like she was dying. How could she find any amusement in that? "You're supposed to say I look beautiful anyway."

He didn't smile, but took a moment to study her no doubt wet and woebegone features. "You look beautiful anyway."

"Liar," she said without spite.

The smile that he sent her was so sweet, her heart would have broken all over again if it wasn't already ripped in two.

"I thought you'd go," she said, after she'd blown her nose and regained a little composure. At least she wasn't leaking salt water like a sieve anymore, although if Eliot wasn't careful, he'd set her off again.

He turned from where he stoked up the fire. She knew that he was granting her some privacy. That was another thing that she'd always appreciated about Eliot. His tact.

Dear God, she needed to stop listing what she liked about Eliot. Better to remind herself of the things she didn't like. To her regret, that boiled down to two things. The fact that he'd set his heart on the preposterous goal of marrying her. And the harrowing truth that they would never come together again after tonight.

Stop it, Verena, or you'll be back to howling like a banshee.

"Do you really want me to go?" he murmured.

No, of course she didn't. "I don't want to fight."

"Neither do I." He glanced at the pretty gold-cased clock on the mantelpiece. "Nobody ever says the right thing at four o'clock in the morning."

He set the poker back in its stand and lifted her heavy velvet peignoir from the chair where her maid had left it. She supposed that after Eliot arrived, Merton must have stopped Celeste from coming up to prepare her for bed. Given what she and Eliot had done in the hallway, that was in every way a good thing.

The girl would appreciate an early night. In a fruitless attempt to divert herself from her sorrow, Verena had been out dancing until dawn every evening this week. Until tonight, when she could no longer summon the will to pretend that she was carefree and heart-whole.

The way things had turned out, she'd have been better off staying at the Plunket ball, where she'd have smiled until her face ached and winced at the false note in her laughter. Although nobody else ever seemed to notice how close she was to breaking.

"Here you are." He set the robe at the base of the bed. Having Eliot pottering around her bedroom once more was so familiar, so pleasant.

Stop it, Verena.

He went across to the decanter set up on the sideboard and poured two glasses of wine, giving her the chance to leave the bed unobserved and wrap the robe around her. As she tied the belt with shaking hands, she realized that he was being tactful again.

When he did marry, as he must, whatever little poppet he chose as his wife would be blessed in her husband. Verena even knew that he'd be faithful to the hussy. He was that sort of man. Once he made a promise, he kept it.

Eliot turned with both glasses in his hands and tilted his square chin toward the upholstered chairs in front of the fire. "I don't want to fight anymore, but can we at least talk like two adults about where we go from here?"

"I don't think we go anywhere," she said in a bleak voice, although she accepted his silent invitation and sat down.

He didn't respond to her statement, although as an intelligent man, he must see that she was right. "I'd at least like the chance to apologize for the way I proposed. I took you by surprise, when I was trying to be romantic. I wanted to sweep you off your feet."

Bitterness rather than genuine amusement dripped from her short laugh. "You'd never even hinted that you weren't satisfied with our arrangement."

As he sat opposite her, his eyes were steady and searching. With the firelight playing over his remarkable features, he looked even more like a man from another age than usual. "Yes, I had."

Yes, he had. Verena recalled the odd humor that he'd been in back in March, when he came to her after returning from the country. That was when everything had changed, after he'd been away from her for a month. That was the first time he'd asked her to drive with him in the park, despite knowing that if they appeared together in public, they'd start every tongue in London wagging.

She thought back to those awful moments at the Lumsden ball. "You know, I owe you an apology, too. I didn't react very graciously."

A rueful curve twisted his lips. "'Thank you, esteemed sir, for your kind attention. While I'm honoured by your generous offer of marriage, I fear I must decline'?"

Again she laughed. Again she was surprised. Nothing about that encounter had ever seemed at all funny before. "I didn't know you read Minerva Press novels."

"I don't, but I've watched that scene at the theater a hundred times. It's always the villain who proposes, while the heroine stays faithful to her true love hovering on the sidelines."

"You're not the villain in this story, Eliot."

"No," he said and took a sip of his wine as he brooded into the blazing fire. The silence lengthened, grew heavy with portent, as if a crowd of ghosts crept closer and closer to hear what came next. Without knowing why, Verena shivered. The room wasn't cold and even if it was, her peignoir kept her warm.

"I'm not the villain." He raised somber gray eyes to study her. "I'm your true love."

CHAPTER TWELVE

*E*liot watched Verena's eyes go wide and dark. He also caught more of that fear he was coming to loathe. Her hand began to shake. "You…"

"It's all right, Verena," he said gently, reaching forward to take her glass and setting it on the small table between the chairs. "You don't have to answer."

She was pale and troubled, but she sat stiff as a ruler in her chair and returned his straight glance with a straight one of her own. He braced for anger, the way that she'd responded to his first proposal with anger.

Whatever she said, it was sure to be a denial. It didn't matter. He was sure that she loved him. He was even sure that she knew it. Although no way in hell was she ever going to admit it.

Her expression remained stern, but he saw the flutter of a pulse in her delicate throat and the way she swallowed before she replied. He waited to hear what a presumptuous devil he was. But what she said surprised him as much as his statement had surprised her.

"Yes, I do love you, Eliot. I don't want to, but plague take you, I can't help it."

By heaven, she was a woman in a million.

He'd never admired her courage more. At his deepest level, he was overjoyed to know that she returned his feelings. Although he'd suspected for a long time that he wasn't the only one enmeshed in emotions that lifted this affair far above mere sensual entertainment.

But more immediate than gratification was his awareness that Verena didn't confess her feelings with any happiness or relief. She spoke the words as if loving him was a curse.

"If you love me—" he began, but she silenced him with a wave of her hand.

"We're not children, and we don't live in fairy land. My love is an inconvenience, and one I intend to conquer."

Her statement elicited a grim smile. "And how do you intend to do that? If you know the secret, I'd love you to share it with me. Because I only find myself more deeply in love with you every day."

His declaration didn't find favor. Her eyes remained lightless, and she turned even paler. "Love doesn't last. It will go away."

"How do you know? Have you been in love before?"

He caught her quick flinch. "No."

"Nor have I. I doubt if it will go away. It certainly hasn't so far. Aren't you a tiny bit tempted to see if we can make a go of things together?"

Before he'd even finished his question, she was shaking her head. Her slender hands shackled the arms of the chair so tight that the knuckles turned white. "I will not marry you, Eliot."

He could tell that she was waiting for him to harangue her the way, God forgive him, he'd harangued her before. Her strength of will shouldn't surprise him. Her unquenchable spirit was one of the many things that he admired about her. If he'd wanted an easy woman to love, he could have chosen one of a thousand others.

Verena wasn't easy. But she was the only one for him.

He kept his voice calm and reasonable. "Tell me why."

She regarded him as if afraid that he played some trick. "You know."

"Give me your reasons for not marrying me, and I'll give you my reasons for why you should."

"You won't change my mind."

"Indulge me." Eliot sat back and extended his bare feet toward the fire. He hadn't got around to putting his shoes on when he'd dressed. "Do you have anything better to do at half past four on a Thursday morning?"

Her dark brown eyebrows arched. She'd got over her crying fit, thank goodness. That had made him feel frantic and guilty and frustrated, because he knew that if he offered comfort, she'd only reject him. "Sleep?"

His grunt expressed wry amusement. "Who needs sleep when there's interesting conversation on offer?"

"Interesting is one way to describe it, I suppose," she responded dryly. "All right, here are my reasons. I hope you won't interrupt me to argue. Or we'll be here into next week."

Eliot gave her a mocking salute, although the threat of staying here with Verena wasn't much of a deterrent. "Aye-aye, Captain."

She cast him an unimpressed glance under her lashes. They'd talked like this so often, with humor overlying serious purpose. This time, his entire happiness depended on the outcome of this discussion. His relaxation was only skin-deep.

"You're a respectable man with a spotless reputation. You're the heir to a great title and a large fortune. You could do much better for a bride than a widow past first youth who promises to be barren. If you wed me, the odds are that there will never be a little Viscount Colville to christen. I didn't conceive when I was married to George, and while I've been careful in the seven years since, accidents happen. But they never seem to happen to me."

She eyed him with more of that wariness, but he kept silent as he'd promised. In truth, he was surprised that she chose her chances of having children as her first point against marrying him. He'd imagined that she'd start with how she refused to entrust herself to another man.

When he didn't object to what she said, she went on. "I've had a thoroughly enjoyable time as a widow. I've taken the men I want as lovers, without giving a fig for what the old tabbies call me. I'm rich and independent and a duke's daughter, which counts for something, however much I despised my father. I might be a bit too outrageous to suit the high sticklers, and I'm not likely to receive a voucher for Almack's any time soon. But most of society is willing to overlook my peccadilloes and continue to associate with me."

All of this sounded as if she argued on his behalf, but he was too smart to fall for that. There was a "but" coming in all this.

Eliot was right. It came in her next sentence.

Her voice hardened. "But you have political ambitions, and Caesar's wife must be above approach. Even if I regretted following my impulses, it's too late to wipe out what I've done since George died. If we wed, people will snigger at your wife –

and also at you for marrying me, when you could have me without a wedding ring. Nobody is going to make the dupe who marries Verena Gerard the country's prime minister. If you take me to wife, you'll have to say goodbye forever to any hope of leaving your mark on public life. It seems a large price to pay, when, as I said, I'm more than willing to share your bed without the church's blessing. You'll have to retire to private life, which would be a pity, because the country's in trouble and there are so few genuinely good men willing to do the work to fix it up."

"England needs me?" he asked in an ironic tone, surprised to find that she took such a broad view of their personal issues. Although he shouldn't be. She came from one of the most powerful families in the land. The Charterises had always played their part in the realm's government.

"Don't you think it does?"

He shrugged and drank a little more of his wine. "I suppose the national crisis is a novel reason for knocking back a fellow's proposal."

"You said you wouldn't interrupt."

"Sorry."

Verena cast him a critical look. "And there's your family. I know you hate your father. Believe me, I can sympathize. But you don't hate Imogen, and I'm not fit company for a pure young girl, especially when she's looking to make a good match. If I'm her sister-in-law, everyone will wonder if I've infected her with my immorality. She deserves better."

Verena stopped and leveled a stark gaze upon him. Her eyes held no hint of hope for a shared future. "So you see, marrying you is out of the question."

He took another sip of his wine. "Am I permitted to speak now?"

"I hope you'll agree with me."

He couldn't help smiling at that. "I'm sure."

Eliot put down his wine and stared into the fire, as he considered his response. This was the fight of his life, and he knew it.

"Those are all fair points," he said slowly, without looking at her. Looking at her played havoc with his ability to put two coherent thoughts together. "Before I refute them, let me be clear about what you're suggesting for us. You're saying that you're content to go back to meeting here on Fridays and sneaking around and pretending we're strangers?"

Verena made a helpless gesture. Her wine remained untouched on the mahogany table. He suspected that she wanted to keep her wits about her. She knew as well as he did that what they said tonight determined their future. "In principle, yes, although we can be a little looser in our arrangements. One afternoon a week isn't enough for me either."

Pleasure squeezed his foolish heart, to hear this confirmation that he hadn't longed alone. "In that case, it will be even harder to keep our affair secret."

She shot him a wry look. "After your recent antics, that's no longer possible. Although perhaps until Imogen marries, we should try to be at least a little discreet. If we're an acknowledged couple, you won't be seen as quite the saint you're proclaimed to be. But you should still be able to play your part in politics. After all, you're hardly the only man in public life with a mistress."

His lips tightened. "It's always struck me as unfair that you've had – what? – not even a dozen lovers, yet you're considered too outré for society's arbiters of morality. While people like my father keep the brothels of London in business, and nobody bats an eyelid at their credentials."

"Five," she said in a small voice.

"Five?"

"Five lovers. Six, if I include you."

Shock slammed through him and made him sit up and stare at her. "I'd heard it was more than that."

"I'm sure you did." Rancor edged her tone. "You know what society is like. The gossips credit me with a different man in my bed every night and two on Sundays. That all sounds like far too much hard work. And anyway, not all my flirtations reached the point of consummation."

Eliot shouldn't be pleased to hear that she hadn't been as profligate as he'd believed. Long ago, he'd come to terms with the fact that Verena had shared her favors with other men before he'd entered her life. He'd found consolation in being damned sure that she hadn't turned to anyone else, since they'd come together.

When he responded, he was very careful to keep his tone neutral. "I should have guessed that the stories were exaggerated. I know men who go through as many different bedmates in a week." Including his father when he was on a spree.

"It's different for women, Eliot. You know that."

"But it's unfair."

"Many things are unfair for women." Her expression remained grave. "I have a name as a depraved hellcat. I'll never shake it, even if I retire to a convent tomorrow and devote the rest of my life to good works."

He made himself smile, although the weary bitterness in her voice told him that she, too, had reflected on how harshly the world judged women who broke the mold. "I hope you're not considering a convent."

"It might save me from another proposal."

"Nonetheless, it's a drastic way to avoid an unwelcome suitor." He paused. "So far, everything you've said sounds reasonable."

He could see that his measured response caught her unprepared. "I'm glad you think so."

"But I'm a man in love. Men in love are never reasonable."

Verena didn't smile. He wished to hell that she took a moment's joy from his love. It only seemed to burden her.

"I think you have to be, Eliot. It's odd, I'd never pictured you as someone prone to grand romantic gestures. You always seem to be the epitome of good sense. Or at least you did." She subjected him to a disapproving inspection. "Although I suppose I should have expected something like this. I've always thought of you as Sir Galahad, and he was definitely a romantic figure."

"I'm no perfect knight."

"You are, you know. And you've set yourself the impossible task of saving the maiden in distress. But I'm not a maiden, and I'm not in distress."

He cast her a long look. "Aren't you?"

She shifted under his piercing stare. To avoid his eyes, at last she lifted her glass to take a sip. "Don't be a fool. You know I'm not."

He didn't know anything of the kind, but he wasn't yet ready to address that particular issue. "So is it my turn to answer your points?"

"If you wish." She didn't sound particularly interested. But of course she'd already made up her mind against marrying him. She was only going through the motions of giving him a chance to persuade her otherwise.

"I do." He ordered his thoughts before he started. "You fear that you can't have children. It's an important issue, or it might be if I cared. But I don't."

"Eliot—"

He raised his hand. "I did you the courtesy of hearing you out. You owe me the same privilege."

Her lips flattened, but she nodded her head as if conceding a point in a fencing match. "I'm sorry. Go ahead."

"Thank you. If you marry me and the Good Lord blesses us with children, I'll be the happiest man in England. If you marry me and we don't have children, I'll still be the happiest man in England, because I'm living with the woman I love. Imogen can't inherit the title, but if she marries and has children, I can leave them my private fortune. As far as the title and the entailed part of my inheritance go, there are plenty of cousins. The Deerforth title doesn't mean much to me, perhaps because it means so much to my father. I certainly don't think the pride of the Ridleys is worth the sacrifice of my every hope of happiness."

Verena shifted again, as if the burden of his love just grew weightier. He imagined it did.

When she didn't interrupt, he went on. "You mention my political career. I don't care about being prime minister. I care about doing something useful with my life and my fortune. Parliament isn't the only avenue of achievement open to a man. When I inherit, I can start with Hamble Park, which my father hasn't run at all as I'd prefer. He thinks the people there exist for his convenience. I don't. And let's face it, I'm only twenty-nine. There's plenty of time to step away from the limelight, then come back later. After you've spent twenty years as a faithful wife, I doubt anyone will give a fig for what you got up to before you saw the light and married me. Even if they do, it will be such old news. A thousand scandals will have come and gone since the remarkable Lady Deerforth kicked up her heels and thumbed her nose at the ton's hypocrisy."

He'd caught her attention now. Those wide, shining blue eyes regarded him as if he belonged to some strange new species. "You must mind that I've taken men other than you into my bed."

Eliot shrugged, not even having to pretend his indifference to what she did before they fell in love. She was the woman he wanted. If he'd wanted an untouched little virgin, there were a hundred that he could choose from, this season alone.

"Must I? I certainly don't want anyone else except me there now, but what you did before we met isn't my concern."

Her mouth crumpled, and for a horrid moment, he feared that she might cry again. But after a visible struggle, she regained her composure, although her voice shook when she spoke. "I don't deserve you, Eliot."

"Of course you do," he said lightly and moved on to his last point. Or his last point to counter her list of reasons against marrying him.

He didn't want to listen to any more claptrap about him being a saint or a perfect knight or Sir Galahad. Verena more than anyone knew that he was as capable of sin as the next man. Especially when given adequate provocation.

"Imogen's stake in this is easy enough to cover. My father says that Lord Halston is about to offer for her. Once she's wed, the gossip about you won't have nearly as much power over her as it does now."

Verena frowned. "Is an engagement so likely between them?"

"According to my esteemed papa, it is. If Imogen marries, you and I will have much more freedom to pursue our joint future."

She didn't look relieved. Instead she looked troubled. "You make a good case. Better than I thought you would."

"I do," Eliot said, although he was a long way from feeling triumphant. Nothing in her voice or manner indicated that he'd won her over. "However, none of that addresses the most powerful thing that stops you agreeing to marry me. The damage that your brute of a husband did to you."

CHAPTER THIRTEEN

Verena's heart slammed hard against her ribs, made her vision go black. She gasped and lurched to her feet, so clumsy with shock that she bumped the table. "Don't..."

The glass tipped over and wine spilled everywhere. "Oh, bother!"

"It's not important," Eliot said, righting the empty glass. "Easy enough to clear up."

She had a sick feeling that he wasn't just talking about the wine puddling over the table and dripping onto the Turkey carpet beneath. If so, he was an optimist. None of this was easy.

He headed for the dressing room, while her shaking hand curled over the edge of the mantel. Her pulses raced, and her legs felt like jelly. So stupid that fear was her principal reaction to Eliot's perception.

Get some control over yourself, Verena.

She wasn't even sure why she was so overcome. After all, Eliot had tried before to discover what had happened in her marriage, and he was smart enough to know that she'd suffered under George's rule.

Perhaps she was so afraid because Eliot saw her too clearly. Those steady gray eyes penetrated the glamorous, self-confident shell of Lady Verena Gerard, who broke men's hearts without a moment's hesitation and who paid no attention to the world's censure.

Those steady gray eyes left her feeling vulnerable and naked. Tonight the cold wind of reality blew around her, and she was afraid that no nice warm blanket of illusion could keep out the chill.

Eliot returned with a bowl of water and a pile of towels and soon had the mess cleaned up. Although she feared that the priceless carpet would bear a permanent stain sure to break Merton's heart anew.

Eliot was a notably capable man. It was something else that she liked about him. With most of her lovers, Verena felt like the adult. That wasn't the case with Eliot. But then, he wasn't like any of the handsome, charming, eminently forgettable men that she'd seduced through her brazen career.

That was the problem.

"Did any splash on your robe?" He kneeled at her feet, doing his best to get the wine out of the carpet. She strove not to remember the last time that he'd kneeled at her feet, when he'd asked her to marry him and destroyed all her hopes of contentment.

Blindly, she glanced down at the thick velvet peignoir. If it was stained, the red material didn't show it. Anyway, the last thing she wanted was his hands on her. Those hands made it so difficult for her to remember life's hard truths. When right now, she needed to remember those truths more than ever.

"No. No, I'm all right," she forced out of a throat pinched so tight that speaking hurt.

"Lucky," he said, rising. He wasn't someone who used his height to dominate, but sometimes like now, she couldn't help noticing what a superb figure of a man he was.

Verena fought back her feminine pleasure in him. That would only weaken her, when she needed to be strong.

Eliot returned to the dressing room to empty out the red-stained water and get rid of the sodden towels. As he left, a bird chirped in the garden outside. Verena couldn't remember the last time that she'd greeted dawn in a lover's presence. Perhaps never. George had always done what he needed to, then returned to his own bed.

A second bird joined in as Eliot came back into the room, stopping in the doorway and studying her with more of that pestilential compassion that made her skin crawl. In an attempt to escape, she edged toward the curtained window.

"Are you going to lie to me and say George's treatment had no effect on you?"

Verena, who had been preparing to do just that, sagged in defeat. "How could it fail to? I was only seventeen when we married and as innocent as a lamb, hard as you'll find that to believe."

"I don't find that hard to believe at all." He didn't smile, although she wanted him to. She did her best to treat her awful marriage with mocking humor. Otherwise, the memories were unendurable.

She sighed, and at last let go of the pretense that she could hide anything from Eliot. He'd always seen too much. Dear God, he'd seen that she loved him, when she'd struggled so hard to keep that secret to herself.

That was yet another reason why she should stay a hundred miles from him. She didn't want anyone to know her so well. "And of course, you're right. He was a brute."

"Of course he was. He hit you, and he bullied you, and he did his best to break your spirit." Eliot's voice was gentle, but she read rage on her behalf in his gray eyes.

She raised her chin and glared at Eliot. "He never did that."

This time, Eliot did smile, a faint curve of his lips, as he stepped further into the room. "No, thank heaven."

"And you won't break me either."

"I don't want to break your spirit, my darling. I want you to be exactly who you are." He spread his hands. "Haven't you realized that yet?"

Everything she knew of the male sex told her that he didn't mean it. "You want to own me."

His smile faded, and his expression turned grave. "I want to love you."

"It's the same thing."

"No, it's not. I'm not George, Verena."

No, he wasn't. He was even more dangerous than George. She'd despised her husband, and she loved Eliot. George had harmed her irreparably, but only Eliot could break her heart.

"You're a good man," she said in a voice weighted with exhaustion. "Too good for me."

Temper lit Eliot's eyes. "Don't start that again."

His anger was so rare that she edged back toward the wall. "I swore when George died that I'd never marry again. I will never break that vow."

His brief flare of rage disappeared under a profound hurt that made her feel like dying. She'd tried to tell herself that his supposed love was a passing fancy, and he'd forget her soon enough, once he no longer shared her bed. When she sent him away, she hadn't caused him any lasting injury.

That, to her bitter regret, had been another comforting lie.

As she beheld Eliot now, she saw so much that she hadn't wanted to see before. So much that she still didn't want to see. But something about this dawn encounter made it impossible to go on deceiving herself.

This man loved her. He loved her with a steady fortitude that made her ache with longing for what he offered. He wouldn't let her down. He wouldn't betray her. He respected her as an equal, which was something new in a lover.

Desire had brought them together. Tonight proved that desire still flared as bright as an exploding star. But the fuel that transformed the physical hunger between them to incandescent flame was love.

Yet, however much she loved him, she couldn't become his wife. For so many reasons. Not least that he deserved better. He was all that was fine, whereas she'd been racing headlong toward perdition since the day her father gave her to that despicable degenerate George Gerard.

And, no, much as she loved Eliot, she didn't want to marry again. Just the thought of placing herself under some man's control tangled her stomach up into knots.

She might be lonely as she was. When Eliot walked away, she'd certainly be devastated. But she was free. And that kept her safe.

Or at least it had, until Eliot bloody Ridley stumbled into her life and made her question decisions that she'd taken years ago.

He must have read refusal in her face. She watched the light fade from his eyes, until he looked old and despairing in a way that she'd never seen before. "You don't trust me," he said, the words toneless with misery.

She wanted to take him in her arms, but that would just extend the agony. "I don't trust myself."

He drew himself up to his full height, and the anguish in his face made her flinch. "You're too afraid to break away from the past. George still holds you prisoner."

She flinched again, because much as she hated to admit it, it was true. When she thought of marriage, the whole world turned dark and threatening. She found it hard to breathe.

No, she couldn't marry anyone. Not even Eliot.

"Eliot, don't ask for so much. Be my lover. Be my friend. But you'll never be my husband. No man will be."

She knew that he'd say no to what she offered. Although she wished to heaven that he wouldn't.

"Verena, we can't go back to where we were a month ago." He sounded as if his last hope had been ripped away. She hated to do this to him. "Too much has happened. Too much has been said. I want to spend the rest of my life with you. I don't want any other woman as my wife."

"We could continue on as lovers."

"It's not enough."

No, she could see that wouldn't be enough for him. Which meant that everything between them was now over. Although stupidly, she persisted in trying to change that conclusion. "It's all I'm offering. Will you at least think about it?"

His lips turned down. "I did think about it before I proposed. I'm greedy, Verena. I want a full life, with you by my side. I want the world to know that we belong to each other. I want you to know that you've found safe harbor in my arms."

Safe harbor. How lovely that sounded. But she was made to wander the lonely oceans alone. Eliot wasn't for her. She was already shaking her head, as a great wedge of painful emotion blocked her throat. "I won't marry you, Eliot. If you can't accept what I'm prepared to give you, we must part."

He still looked desolate. She tried to tell herself that it was better this way, rather than letting the affair peter out into recriminations and bitterness and resentment. Because in the end, he'd be angry with her for not giving him what he wanted. He was a man, after all.

"So what happens now?"

She tried to smile, but her trembling lips wouldn't hold the curve. "We go back to where we were before we came together, although I suspect that your reputation as a saint might show a few cracks."

He didn't smile either. The lines between his nose and mouth were etched deep, and an unhappy furrow marked that noble forehead. "So you'll take another man into your bed."

She shrugged, although careless was the last thing she felt. "It's what I do."

His dark gold eyebrows lowered in a scowl. "Shelburn, I suppose."

"That's none of your concern." Right now, the idea of starting another affair held no appeal, but perhaps a new lover might distract her from her heartache. Because she had no doubt that she'd miss Eliot like the devil. These last few weeks without him had been purgatory. She dreaded to think what this new goodbye was going to cost her in tears and futile longing and sleepless nights.

"You're letting your fear win, Verena." He studied her. Nobody had ever seen her so clearly. It amazed her that, seeing her so clearly, he still loved her. "I'd thought better of you."

Her hand sliced the air in a disconsolate gesture. "Better I disappoint you now than when you've pledged your life to me. Go back to your world, Eliot. You never really belonged in mine. I certainly never belonged in yours. Let's kiss and part."

"Very well." He stepped forward and caught her hard by the shoulders. She braced for an angry farewell, but when he kissed her, the contact was gentle and sad and sweet.

With a sigh that was burdened with a lake of unshed tears, she closed her eyes and yielded. As long as she lived, she'd carry the poignant memory of this tenderness with her.

His mouth pursued its soft exploration. His scent made her head swim. As heat rose and teased her senses, shaking hands clutched at his back. She pressed closer, feeling Eliot's body stir.

Just as she wondered whether perhaps they'd end up back in her bed one more time, he drew away. "Think of me, Verena," he murmured and turned to pick up his shoes and walk out of the room.

The soft bump of the door shutting behind him sounded like a death knell.

CHAPTER FOURTEEN

When scandal finally broke, as it was sure to, it emerged from an unexpected direction.

The storm of gossip that engulfed the Ridley family had nothing to do with Eliot's interest in George Gerard's widow. Instead, it blew up because of his father, Imogen, Lord Halston, and most surprising of all, his self-effacing cousin, Stella Faulkner.

Halston hadn't been pursuing Imogen at all, despite the rumors. Rumors that were in many cases founded on Lord Deerforth's confident assertions to all and sundry that his daughter was about to become the next Countess of Halston.

Instead, it turned out that Halston's interest had always been fixed on Imogen's governess. His lordship and Stella had fallen in love without attracting the ton's attention.

The marriage of one of London's most eligible bachelors to a penniless governess with a shady background would have set tongues wagging anyway. Throw in the humiliation of Lord Deerforth, and however innocent she might be in the affair, his daughter, plus whispers of some fracas at the Lorimer Square house where Deerforth and Halston almost came to blows, and the whole situation provided irresistible fodder for tattle.

Eliot accepted an invitation to Stella's wedding and because he was the only member of the Ridley family present, he agreed to give her away. For quite a while, he'd felt guilty about leaving his cousin in his father's bullying charge.

Now that he had an opportunity to take Lord Halston's measure, he found himself unexpectedly impressed. Although he couldn't help observing the happy couple with a fair measure of envy. Their mutual love and happiness were palpable. It was what he'd dreamed of finding with Verena.

His head told him that there was no use in pursuing his headstrong lady further. She'd decided against him and wouldn't change her mind.

His foolish, faithful heart couldn't give up all hope of ever making her his. He supposed that, under the terms of his agreement with his father, he was now free to court Verena. He'd promised to refrain from causing talk until Halston and Imogen had sorted things out between them. Unexpected as the denouement proved to be, that particular issue had reached its end.

If only that made a difference to Eliot's chances with his beloved.

The day after his cousin's wedding, Eliot called on the Lorimer Square house. Imogen's season had come to a disastrous end. Word of the ructions among the Ridleys had been out since last week, when Deerforth had bellowed his outrage without thought of who might hear him.

The nastier members of the ton, jealous of Imogen's social success, were even now twisting the truth to say that she'd made a blatant play for Lord

Halston and she deserved her downfall. Eliot was sure that within a week, poor Imogen would be spoken of as a greedy harpy with ambitions far beyond her reach.

Yet to Eliot's surprise, his sister didn't look particularly cast down when he met her in the house's elegant morning room, with its view over the back garden, bright with spring flowers.

"Are you all right?" he asked, once they were alone together with the tea tray.

His father, to his relief, wasn't home. Lord Deerforth had hunkered down at his club to escape the uproar. This afternoon, he wouldn't barge in and somehow manage to make this mess all Eliot's fault, as was his habit.

"Perfectly all right, although I'm sorry that I have to go back to Hamble Park in disgrace."

Lord Deerforth was packing Imogen up and sending her back to Gloucestershire. Her season was over for this year, at least. Perhaps by next year, all this brouhaha would be forgotten and his sister could make a fresh start in society.

"I'm sorry you've been dragged into this. You didn't do anything wrong. If Father had an ounce of sense, he'd have kept his blasted trap shut."

Imogen's smile was rueful, as she sat on the chaise longue near the French windows and sipped her tea. "I mightn't have done anything wrong, but people are still laughing at me. They say that I'm the girl fool enough to imagine that she'd caught the elusive Lord Halston, then found herself having to stomach her cousin marrying him instead."

"I loathe society's spite."

Imogen shrugged. If she was crushed under romantic disappointment, she was doing a good job of hiding it. "People always love to talk."

"It's not so nice when they're talking about you."

"It's not. But I doubt my reputation will be in the doldrums forever."

"Do you mind very much?"

"That Stella married Halston? Not at all. They're so very much in love, and he wouldn't have suited me at all."

Eliot couldn't doubt that she meant it. Relieved, he relaxed back in his chair and finished his cup of tea. "I'm so glad your heart isn't broken. I feared it might be."

Imogen responded to that idea with a dismissive laugh. "Goodness me, no. Although I might have married Halston to get my claws into the grounds at Prestwick Place. They make Hamble Park look like a wasteland."

If Imogen was back talking about gardens, her forthcoming exile hadn't hit her too badly. "You'll get a chance to finish your parterre now."

"Yes, and Papa is feeling so guilty about spoiling my season, he's agreed to let me build a lake. Or a large pond, at least. I also won't have to dance with Lord Chippenham, just to keep Papa from nagging me. London will still be waiting next year. I imagine by then, nobody will care that I'm the girl Lord Halston overlooked."

Eliot leveled a searching look upon her. "You're being very sensible about all this."

Surprisingly so. Since she'd come to London, his sister had changed. He supposed that she'd had a chance to find her feet. It was difficult to recall the rather childish moping that she'd indulged in at first, when she'd been so homesick. Now it appeared that she was ready to weather a major scandal without turning a hair.

Imogen waved away the compliment. "What choice do I have?"

Eliot smiled. "None, I suppose. But you're still impressing the life out of me, sis."

As she replaced her teacup on the tray, she shot Eliot a sharp glance. "Speaking of broken hearts, my dear brother, you're looking rather gaunt."

"Late nights of political discussion," he said with a lightness that he didn't feel. He was sure that the time would come when he'd manage to speak of Verena without feeling like he was being ripped into bloody gobbets. But just now, his failure in love was still too fresh.

"I like Verena."

Eliot bit back a sigh. Despite his lack of encouragement, Imogen meant to persist in inquiring after his well-being. "Yes."

"And so do you." Imogen paused, and Eliot realized with a shock that the little sister he'd loved and protected and patronized no longer existed. This was a young woman with decided opinions and a surprising amount of acumen. "In fact, you love her. Are you going to marry her?"

To his surprise, he found himself answering honestly. "She won't have me."

If he'd been less heartbroken, he might have found it in him to appreciate Imogen's unhidden incredulity at that statement. "But she loves you, too."

Yes, Verena did, but that only made her more determined to refuse Eliot's proposal. "She doesn't think we'd suit."

"Then she's silly."

Despite his wretchedness, Eliot couldn't help laughing at that. "There speaks the fond sister."

"Nonetheless, it's true. You're a good man with a kind heart. That's rare enough to make you a catch, apart from the fact that all the girls sigh over how handsome you are."

"All the girls, apart from the one girl I want, to my regret," he said with a trace of bitterness.

"I suppose that she's worried about causing a scandal. Everybody says that she's wild and wanton, and you're touted as a future prime minister."

"I don't care about a scandal," he said grimly.

Imogen's smile conveyed a genuine compassion that made him shift in discomfort. "What about your political career?"

"That was always Father's plan for me. I went along with it because it seemed a suitable use for my time and talents, but it's time I forged my own destiny."

"With Lady Verena?"

"I said that she'd refused me."

Imogen shook her head, as if she was disappointed in him. "Eliot, you're not a man to give up at the first hurdle."

Self-deprecation twisted his lips. "She's refused me several times. She doesn't wish to marry."

"Even though she loves you?"

"Does she?"

"When I saw you together, she looked to me like she did."

"Whether she does or she doesn't, she's adamant that she won't become my wife."

Imogen remained unconvinced. "You've won so many victories in parliament when everyone said that a solution was impossible. You're thinking like a man in love and not a politician."

Startled, he studied Imogen. "I love Verena dearly, but she's right that there will be an avalanche of talk if we wed. Don't you mind?"

With a laugh, Imogen batted away his question. "Right now, the family name is mired in scandal. What difference will a little more gossip make?"

Eliot couldn't help smiling back. Her time in London had given her a sophistication that he'd never imagined his garden-mad sister developing. "Get it all out of the way at once?"

"Why not?" Imogen's voice lowered into seriousness. "If you love Verena and Verena loves you, it would be a crime to let that hope of happiness slip through your fingers. Love is too precious to waste."

"When did you become so wise?"

She made a dismissive gesture. "I've always been wise. You've just been too wrapped up in playing my lordly older brother to notice."

"We caught the nice weather," Verena said, as she and Shelburn drove under the arching trees in Hyde Park. This Friday afternoon, the park was almost empty. It was too early for the fashionable hour, which suited Verena. She wanted privacy for what she planned to say to the earl. "Thank you for taking me out in your carriage today."

She'd been desperate to get out of her house. At home, she was too aware that for most of the last year, her Friday afternoons had belonged to Eliot.

Last Friday afternoon, she'd moped around like a sick cat. She refused to do that ever again. For heaven's sake, she was the fascinating Verena Gerard. No man could bring her down. She was tired of feeling sorry for herself. It was bad for her complexion.

Yesterday, she'd sent a note around to Shelburn, asking him if he'd like to take her driving. She'd had a disappointment in love. It happened to everyone. She wasn't going to let losing Eliot color the rest of her life in dour shades of mourning.

She'd shone for the last seven years. She'd go on shining.

"Well, you asked me." Shelburn's glance was sardonic. "I could hardly say no to an old friend, could I?"

Her lips firmed with resentment. He didn't need to make it sound like she'd begged him. "I had something particular to talk about," she said, curling her hand around his arm in a way that she hoped would give him a clue to where her thoughts were heading.

"Oh?" Shelburn said, drawing the horses back to a gentle amble. "Something you can't say at the Chastain ball tonight, when I believe we're engaged for a waltz and a quadrille?"

She frowned, then smoothed her expression to a smile. Shelburn wasn't acting much like a swain, but she could change that, she was sure. He just hadn't guessed what she was about to offer him. "I don't want anyone listening. You know how the ton like to talk."

"I do indeed." He pulled the horses to a stop and turned to face her, breaking her hold on his arm. "Spill it, Verena. What is all this about? Since I collected you, you've been positively kittenish. What the devil are you up to?"

She struggled with the urge to box his ears. She'd done that once when she was a girl, after he'd teased her without mercy about a fussy new bonnet that the twelve-year-old Verena had just adored.

"Kittenish?" she asked, trying not to sound annoyed.

He nodded, dark eyes amused beneath the brim of his stylish high-crowned hat. "Kittenish. I was wondering if I should stop at Gunter's and request a bowl of milk for my companion." He studied her with closer attention. "Actually, some milk or something equally fortifying might be just the thing for you. You're looking decidedly peaked. Almost haggard."

"That's not very gallant," she snapped, before she reminded herself that a squabble wouldn't advance her cause.

She'd hoped the rouge pot and some red lip salve might hide the signs of wear that she'd seen in her mirror when she dressed. That, and the dashing scarlet carriage dress that had always been one of her favorites.

It seemed that she'd hoped in vain.

He shrugged. "With a childhood chum, I'm not going to waste time on lying flattery."

"I think I'd prefer lying flattery to brutal frankness," she said dryly.

"Then you've changed." Disbelief arched his eyebrows. "I've always admired your courage and your willingness to face up to life's harder realities."

She caught her breath at the unexpected compliment and smothered the reluctance that had weighted her stomach since she'd decided to follow this path. Once perhaps, she'd been brave, as Shelburn had called her. At this moment, she fought the urge to pack herself away in a dark room and never come out again.

Verena steeled herself to proceed. Shelburn had given her the perfect opening.

She summoned what was left of her failing determination and lifted her chin, sending him what she hoped was a glance loaded with sultry appeal. "I'm sure that you admire more about me than that. I'm sure in fact that you're wondering, as I always have, why you and I haven't ever ended up in bed together. We get along so well. We've flirted for years. I find you very attractive, and you've always given every sign that you're attracted as well. It's time we did something about that, don't you agree?"

There. She'd done it.

She'd started her recovery from the madness that had descended on her when she took up with Eliot. Why, after a month of Shelburn as her lover, she'd barely remember who Eliot Ridley was. By all reports, Shelburn was a passionate and inventive partner in bed sport.

Whenever she'd invited a man to be her lover in the past, he'd responded with overjoyed enthusiasm. Although it was more usual for gentlemen to make the proposition and leave the acceptance to Verena. In those cases, her agreement resulted in gratitude as well as anticipation.

Shelburn, the villain, reacted with neither joy nor gratitude. Instead, he regarded her with a thoughtful coolness that made her hands clench around the red silk reticule resting in her lap. "Are you asking me to sleep with you, Verena?"

What else? Had he suddenly lost his ability to understand English? "Yes."

This wasn't going as she'd planned. She'd imagined an acknowledged rake like Shelburn would leap at the offer of an affair.

"I'm sorry, my dear, but I don't think we would suit. I've known you since you were in your cradle. I feel like your brother."

How very awkward. It turned out that if the scoundrel was leaping anywhere, he was leaping away from her. Verena began to wish that she'd never started this and she'd chosen some other gentleman to eradicate her obsession with Eliot. Except that nobody else appealed to her at all.

If she was brutally honest, Shelburn didn't appeal to her either. Not in that way.

But at least she liked him and trusted him, and a liaison with such a noted rake would confirm that she was the comely widow, able to make a claim on any attractive man she wanted. She was desperate to remind herself and the world that she was a rapacious seductress.

To her annoyance, Shelburn didn't look seduced. In fact, he looked almost as uncomfortable as she felt.

"But you're not my brother," she said in a cutting tone, before she remembered that she meant to sound alluring.

Shelburn released a heavy sigh and reached across to take her gloved hand. Not, she suspected, as the prelude to touching any of the more intimate parts of her body. "Verena, we've always been such good friends. Why spoil that with asking for anything further? Women willing to come to my bed are ten a penny. But I can count my genuine friends on one hand. And I include you in that number."

"Friendship doesn't stop us being lovers," she said with a hint of desperation that she feared he might hear. If he did, that would just be the utter end of enough. "It adds an extra dimension to the association."

"Perhaps," he said gently, squeezing her hand in a damnably fraternal fashion. "You're a beautiful woman. And smart. And witty. And interesting."

"None of those sound like compliments," she said in a flat voice.

He smiled at her with the fondness that she'd always relied upon. Fondness, but not a hint of desire, curse him. "That's a pity, because they are."

"Are you saying no to my offer?" she asked, although she already knew the answer.

"I'm very flattered that you thought of me, my lady." He raised her hand and kissed her knuckles through her red glove. "But I'm afraid that it just won't do."

Verena was tired and on edge. And she'd already spent too much time crying. Nonetheless, hot tears pricked at her eyes. Mainly pique, but injured feelings were present, too. "We could be marvelous together."

"No, we couldn't." His rueful smile deepened. "And you know that as well as I do."

"No, I don't." Plague take him, her voice was cracking. If she wasn't careful, she'd start blubbering like an abandoned infant any moment now. She snatched a shaky breath and struggled for composure. "I don't know that at all."

"Yes, you do." Shelburn's eyes were kind. She was getting vastly sick of kind men. "If I take a mistress, I want her to be devoted to me alone. At least while the affair lasts."

"I'm always faithful to my lovers. You know that."

"I do. And I know if you come to my bed, you won't stray. But you'll still be in love with Eliot Ridley, and I don't want a mistress who's pining for another man when I'm doing my best to keep her entertained."

"I'm not..." she began in shock, then she let her appalled protest peter out to silence. Shelburn was watching her with too much understanding for her to have a prayer of convincing him that he was wrong.

"I don't want to be in love with Eliot." She tugged her hand free of his and buried it in her skirts to hide its trembling. "I don't want to be in love with anyone."

The compassion in Shelburn's smile made her bridle with resentment. All her life, she'd loathed pity. The idea that someone who knew her so well should feel sorry for her made her want to hit something. Her preference would be Eliot, but he'd never again be within reach.

"I'm sure that's true, but it happens to most of us. I must say I'm surprised that after all these years of roués and cads, you're enamored of someone so respectable. Although I suppose if you were likely to fall for a roué or a cad, you'd have done it before now."

"There's nothing between Eliot and me," Verena said, hating how that admission flooded her with misery.

"He likes you. He must. Or he wouldn't have made such an exhibition of himself, chasing you these last few weeks. Why not make a play for him? If you want him, have him. It's what you usually do."

She sat up straight and glared at Shelburn. "As you have refused my invitation to become my lover, you have no right to an opinion on my private life. Please take me home. I find myself rather fatigued, and as you pointed out, the Chastain ball is tonight. I've been told that I need to catch up on some sleep if I want to look my best."

Her spiky response only made Shelburn laugh, which didn't put her any more in charity with him. "That's the way. Come out fighting. Although, damn me, I can't work out why a bonny fighter like you isn't fighting for the man she wants, instead of fighting with the man she doesn't want. Makes no sense, Verena."

Her glare sharpened. "Have you finished making obnoxious remarks, my lord?"

Her set-down didn't quash his effrontery. Why would it? In all their years of acquaintance, she'd never managed to gain the upper hand over Shelburn. "Very well. I'll pull my head in and let you gallop headlong to hell in your own way. But when you're nursing a broken heart, don't cut up rough if I say I told you so."

"I have no heart. Don't you know that?" She stopped looking at him and stared over the horses' heads. "I'm untamed, reckless Verena Gerard, who allows no man dominion over her and who does whatever she pleases."

The acid note in her voice gave away how upset she was. Although what she said had once been true. As with so much else in her life, Eliot had destroyed her freedom, too. If she didn't love him so much, she'd hate him.

Shelburn clicked his tongue to his chestnuts to move them on. His voice was soft, as he responded to her shaky defiance. "You might try and make the rest of the world believe you're hard and uncaring, my girl, but you can't pull the wool over my eyes. Your problem has always been too much heart rather than not enough."

Verena didn't reply. Partly because she was terrified that he was right. When too much heart had only caused her endless trouble.

CHAPTER FIFTEEN

Shelburn pulled his carriage up in front of Verena's house. He leaped down to come around and help her down, as a footman ran out to hold the horses. "Are we still going to dance together tonight, Verena, or are we at outs after today?"

She cast him a cold look. "Whatever you wish."

He bowed with a flourish. "You'll forgive me in the end. You don't hold a grudge."

"Don't I?" she said in a neutral tone. "We'll see."

"You don't want me. You know you don't. Why not go for what you really want?"

"And why don't you mind your own business?"

Her sniffy response made him laugh. He knew he was out of favor, but he also knew that like him, she didn't have enough old friends to discard one of them just because she was in a huff.

Right now, she felt embarrassed and annoyed that he'd had the temerity to refuse her. But her pride wouldn't let her reveal the wound that he'd dealt to her vanity. She raised her chin and pulled her hand free of his. "Thank you for taking me driving, my lord."

"It was my pleasure, my dear."

"I'm obviously not your dear," she said, her cheeks stiff with keeping her insouciant smile.

"Yes, you are."

"As a brother."

"I've been a better brother to you than either of your actual brothers."

Even after today's mess, that was true, but she wasn't yet willing to admit that. "That's not saying much." The chestnuts shifted and scraped their hooves against the road. "Your horses are eager to go. You shouldn't keep them standing."

"No, I shouldn't." He bowed again. "Good afternoon, Verena. I'll see you this evening."

She didn't wait to watch him drive away. Instead she climbed the steps to where Merton held the door open. Then she proceeded up the staircase to the bedroom that it seemed she'd never share with Shelburn. She'd denied Eliot access, and Shelburn didn't want her. At this rate, she'd be celibate until Christmas.

Celeste was waiting to help her change out of her carriage dress. The maid slid a loose muslin robe over Verena's shoulders. The day was too warm for the velvet peignoir. "I'd like to rest before I dress for dinner."

"*Oui, madame,*" Celeste said. "Let me take down your hair."

"Thank you." She perched on her dressing stool, as her maid unpinned the stylish chignon and began to brush it out. Verena closed her eyes and let the soporific rhythm of the hairbrush soothe her jangling nerves.

Curse Shelburn. How dare he turn her down? How dare he give her advice? How dare he pretend to have some insight into her heart?

Verena was miffed, and her pride stung like blazes. But as she opened her eyes and studied her face in the mirror, she couldn't help but admit that her principal emotion was relief.

She was glad that she wasn't going to take Shelburn as her paramour. She was glad that she didn't have to go through the same, tired old dance with a new lover. At least not straightaway.

How lowering to realize that right now, unless Eliot was in her bed, she'd rather occupy it alone.

Dear Lord, was she getting too old for the games that she'd played since George's death? Had she lost the thrill that she'd always felt when she broke every rule set down for well-bred young ladies?

She was thirty, after all. Perhaps it was time to find new challenges, new goals.

But what?

If she put away her life of sin and glamour, what was left? Yet was there any point in acting the wicked widow, if her antics gave her no enjoyment?

Shelburn had mentioned that she looked drained. He was right, devil take him. Her hair was still thick and shining, her skin still creamy and firm, her body curved and graceful. But when she looked into her eyes, the light had gone out of them. She looked like a woman suffering a secret sorrow. In a subtle way, she looked much older than her years. And she had a nasty suspicion that over time, that change would become less subtle, as discontent and loneliness ate at her vitality.

Was it time for a change? Was it time to stop kicking against her dead father and her dead husband to prove that she'd won and they'd lost? She was alive, which was surely her greatest revenge on both of those monsters.

Was it time to put the anger and pain of the past behind her? Was it time to grow up at last?

On Saturday afternoon during fashionable hour, Eliot took the grays into the park. It felt odd not to see Imogen out enjoying the fresh air, too, but by now, she was safely back in Gloucestershire.

Verena didn't appear to be present. He'd looked for her at the Chastain ball last night, but hadn't seen her then either. Shelburn had been there, flirting with all the debutantes, the rogue. So at least Eliot hadn't had to imagine his rival rolling about in Verena's bed.

Although he supposed that he shouldn't feel too reassured. The bastard could have gone to Verena, once the party finished.

Imogen's encouragement had rung in his ears since he'd called to say goodbye to her. She'd seemed to think that he had a chance with his beloved. Although his sister had no idea of the complicated history of his courtship.

She'd accused him of giving up on Verena too soon. Damn him if he didn't think that she had a point. He'd schemed and negotiated and maneuvered with his parliamentary colleagues to get what he wanted. He wanted Verena more than he'd ever wanted anything else in his life. If he used his brain, surely he could work out how to win her.

And she loved him. That must give him some advantage. She didn't want to care, but she couldn't help herself. He just had to arrange things so that she could no longer bear to say no.

"Good afternoon, Colville," Shelburn said from just behind him.

Eliot started, giving the reins a jerk that made his skittish horses whinny and toss their heads. He'd taken their measure by now, but he never underestimated how highly strung they were.

"Shelburn," he said without pleasure.

The earl was on foot and looking his usual superior self. The urge to smash that smug smile from the fellow's face was nigh irresistible. Eliot gave a brief bow, searching the area for Verena. Lately the two had been inseparable in public.

"The park is busy today, isn't it? I'll swear it gets worse every year."

Puzzled, Eliot regarded his rival. The man appeared to be in the mood for conversation, which was the last thing that Eliot wanted. "Yes."

"The Chastain affair was a bear's den last night, too, wasn't it?"

"Yes." Eliot was desperate to come out with something haughty and crushing, but he seemed to be stuck agreeing with the swine.

Who studied the grays with an acquisitive light in his eyes. "I envy you those high steppers. I wish I'd seen them first."

"Well, you didn't," Eliot said shortly, although the riposte hardly stretched to the definitive set-down that he burned to come up with.

"Would you consider selling them? They're the nicest nags I've seen in a dog's age."

Ah, that explained Shelburn's sudden interest in talking to him. He wanted to get his grubby hands on the grays. "Why would I sell them? I think they're a wonderful pair, too."

"Pity. I'd pay over the odds."

Then like a sky full of fireworks bursting inside his head, Eliot came up with an idea. A rather bold and improper idea, and one that he knew would make Verena furious. But if Verena was furious, at least she was thinking about him.

Imogen had told him to start working strategically. Imogen was right. At this moment, Eliot had something that Shelburn wanted, and Shelburn had something that Eliot wanted. Perhaps they could arrange a trade.

He turned to face Shelburn and smiled down at him with a grin that he feared might look rather wolfish. Shelburn had no idea what he was about to take on. "You know, I've often wondered how they'd go against those pretty chestnuts of yours."

"A race?" Shelburn regarded him with a hint of wariness. The man might be a blackguard, but he was no fool.

"Yes. If you come in first, you can have the grays. It will be cheaper than buying them."

Shelburn frowned. "And you get my chestnuts if you win?"

Eliot was so pleased with himself that he laughed. "What the devil do I want with your chestnuts, man? No, there's something else I want from you."

Shelburn's eyebrows arched in inquiry. "And what's that?"

Verena would never forgive him for what he was about to do, by God. But the chance was too tempting to pass up. "You've established an arrangement with Lady Verena Gerard."

Surprise lit Shelburn's eyes. What an idiot the man was if he imagined that Verena's preference for his company hadn't attracted society's notice. "Have I indeed?"

"That's the talk anyway." Eliot inhaled to firm his purpose, although his mind was already made up. "If I win the race, you will surrender any claim on Lady Verena and break off all contact."

"By contact, you mean..."

"Devil take you, you know exactly what I mean. The affair ends when I cross the winning line ahead of you."

"And has the lady any say in this?"

"She's only passing the time with you."

Shelburn looked amused rather than offended. "Perhaps that's true, but if she and I are no longer together, that doesn't mean she'll turn to you instead."

"What happens afterward is none of your concern."

"If I win, I'll get my clutches on the grays *and* Verena."

"You're not going to win, Shelburn." Eliot's vitriolic hatred for this self-satisfied weasel deepened. "In the race or in love."

"Ah, it's love, is it?" Shelburn responded on a mocking note. "In that case, it would be ungallant not to play the game."

"Good show," Eliot said equally dryly. "When are you at leisure?"

"Tomorrow? It's Sunday, and the traffic shouldn't be as bad as on a weekday."

While Eliot and Shelburn negotiated the terms of their wager, people had stopped to listen to their discussion. Eliot didn't care. Now that Imogen's marriage prospects were no longer at issue, he didn't care if the whole world knew about his interest in Verena. He could ignite scandals left, right and center, if the fancy took him.

One thing was for sure. This race would set off a huge brouhaha. If Eliot participated, even more if he won, nobody would ever again accuse him of being old before his time.

"Suits me," Eliot bit out. "A twenty-mile course? Anything much further than that and we'll have to change horses, when the whole point is to put our cattle through their paces.”

Shelburn might be a famous whip, but Eliot was no slouch either and he'd back his grays against any team in England. Not to mention that his frustrated love gave him added incentive to win. Shelburn might desire Verena, but he didn't love her. If he did, he wouldn't risk losing her like this, no matter how much he coveted Eliot's horses.

“That sounds good. It's twenty miles from Islington to Hatfield. If we leave from Mayfair, we'll spend hours getting out of Town, even on a Sunday.”

“Very well. You're on. The Angel through to the Greyhound,” Eliot said, naming two well-known coaching inns. “Eight tomorrow morning.”

“So deuced early?” Shelburn reacted with theatrical horror. “I head off to bed around then.”

“If you'll take my advice, you'll get a good night's sleep beforehand. You're not going to win, but I'd hate you to put up a poor show.”

Eliot's insincere concern made Shelburn laugh. “Hark at your confidence, Colville. I'll almost be sorry to leave you choking on my dust. Be damned to you, eight tomorrow it is. I'll ask Freddie Edgecombe to go to the Greyhound ahead of us to witness the finish. Although he'll curse me for keeping him from his bed at that hour on a Sunday morning.”

“And I'll ask Anthony Comerford to be my witness.”

Shelburn's expression conveyed an injury as insincere as Eliot's concern. “Don't you trust me?”

Not as far as I can kick you, you woman-stealing mongrel. Eliot kept his smile in place. “How could I not?”

“Capital. I'll let my head groom know that we're about to take on two more horses. He'll love getting his hands on those grays. Tomorrow morning, you'll make both of us the happiest of men, my lord."

Over my dead body, you toadying scoundrel. "We'll see tomorrow, won't we?"

Curiosity buzzed around them. The crowd of eavesdroppers had swelled with astonishing speed. Verena would hear of the wager within the hour, if Eliot was any judge of the speed that gossip traveled in the ton.

He probably should mind how livid she'd be, once she discovered that he and Shelburn had bandied her name about in public. But right now, the prospect of grinding his competitor's face into the mud was too alluring for him to have attention left for much else.

"We will indeed. I look forward to showing you what a master can do with the ribbons," Shelburn said.

Eliot bared his teeth at his rival. "And I look forward to greeting you with a tankard of ale when you arrive at the Greyhound behind me."

CHAPTER SIXTEEN

*E*ven before eight on a Sunday morning, the Angel at Islington was crowded and bustling. Some coaches still ran, despite it being the Sabbath, and private travelers were always on the move. Not to mention that news of the race between the scandalous Lord Shelburn and the once-respectable Lord Colville to win the favors of Lady Verena Gerard had spread far and wide.

Despite the unsociable hour, many members of the ton had gathered in Islington after their Saturday night revels, instead of seeking their beds. The contest promised grand entertainment, especially on such a beautiful day.

When Eliot emerged from the stables where he'd been giving the grays a last check, he was astonished to witness the hubbub. The yard was jammed. Curious onlookers in rough garb mixed with highborn lords in evening dress, and quite a few ladies in silk gowns mingled with the crowd.

"Good Lord, what's this?" he asked in bewilderment. He'd stayed overnight at the Angel, so his horses were well rested and didn't have to cover the four miles from London before he set them galloping to Hatfield.

"It's like a bloomin' Christmas fair," Grimes, his groom, said in disapproval from where he sat beside Eliot in the sporting curricle. Grimes would follow him to Hatfield to take charge of the horses after the race. That was if Eliot won. He hoped to hell he won.

The grays didn't like all this hullabaloo. They snorted and tossed their heads and stamped their feet.

"Easy, my beauties," Eliot said, bringing them back under control. The last thing he needed was for his cattle to trample some reckless pedestrian.

He tipped his hat to Shelburn in a mocking salute. His rival's carriage was on the opposite side of the yard, mobbed by well-wishers. All around, Eliot saw money changing hands. There seemed to be a rash of betting on the race's outcome.

"Cor, my lord," Tom said in admiration, as he ran out of the crowd to hold the horses' heads. He'd travel to Hatfield with Grimes. "You've set the cat among the bleedin' pigeons with this race. I just heard some swell cove put five hundred guineas on Lord Shelburn for the win."

Eliot couldn't help smiling at his tiger's enthusiasm, although for him, the outcome of this race was as serious as life and death. "Is anyone betting on me?"

"A few natty morts who have spied the grays in Hyde Park. But the odds are on Lord Shelburn. He's known as a great whip, and until now, you've hidden your light under a bushel."

"Good for the natty morts," Eliot said dryly. He hoped that they were natty enough to be right about him coming in first, or he'd end the day deprived of both horses and Verena.

"I put two bob on you, my lord," Tom said loyally, gazing up at Eliot from under an untidy thatch of straw-colored hair. His expression said that he couldn't imagine anyone ever besting his master.

"And I put a crown on you, too, sir," Grimes said in his characteristic flat voice. "Nobody handles the ribbons like you do, as I know, even if the world doesn't. And those grays are the best runners I've seen in forty years of working with horses. Lord Shelburn's good, but he's flashy. You'll come out ahead, my lord, and I'm willing to lay out hard-earned brass to show you how sure I am of that."

"Thank you, both of you. I'm dashed grateful." Touched by their stalwart support, Eliot smiled at his servants. "In that case, I'd better make sure I win."

A couple of acquaintances called out greetings and he responded, but his mind was on the contest to come. "Let them go, Tom. I need to line up next to Shelburn."

"Good luck, my lord," Tom said.

"Thank you, lad."

"Godspeed, my lord," Grimes said, touching his hat in a respectful salute before he climbed down.

"Make way for his lordship. Make way," the boy shouted, walking ahead and clearing a path through the throng.

Rising excitement charged the air. Eliot had entered this race with a grim sense of fatalism. As if he made one final despairing roll of the dice to recoup his fortunes, on a night when luck hadn't run his way. But even his overburdened heart rose at the prospect of a good run on such a bright morning.

Thank heaven it wasn't raining. Bad weather wouldn't just make the trip unpleasant. Slippery roads presented a danger to his team. Even on the best days, it was perilous to dash all out along the Great North Road. Accidents were a daily occurrence.

The vociferous crowd parted just enough for him to maneuver his rig next to Shelburn's. It was the high-perch phaeton that he'd seen before, not least on that humiliating day when Verena had left him behind on her steps while she drove off with his rival.

"Good morning, Shelburn." He had to raise his voice over the clamor of the earl's supporters. The representatives of high society who turned up this morning were mostly from the wilder element. Shelburn was much more popular with them than Eliot, who until recently had borne a reputation as a bit of a dry stick, he knew.

By God, he'd well and truly smashed that over these last weeks, hadn't he? The world might now dismiss him as a reckless fool, but nobody would ever again call him a self-righteous bore.

Somewhere in Mayfair, his father would be stamping around with steam coming out of his ears. Eliot had no doubt that the Pater would have heard about this latest example of the way his son had started thumbing his nose at propriety.

He grinned at the man who he intended to trounce without mercy today. "Are you ready to lose the race?"

Shelburn laughed. "Good morning, Colville. You're brimming with vinegar this morning. Almost makes me sad that I'm going to beat you. Such a pity to dash hopes that have risen so unreasonably high."

"Your horses have already come from London, so the advantage is mine." Eliot watched Tom take the grays' heads again, as they showed their discontentment with the crescendo of noise and the chaotic movement whirling around them.

"Not at all, old man. My cattle spent a good night in the stables here under my groom's supervision. I however have just come from Town.

You missed a good night at the Brices'. The ball was a crush and didn't finish until nearly four. I vow I'll enjoy seeing my bed, once all this tomfoolery is over."

Eliot did his best to hide his annoyance. Shelburn could at least make a show of caring about the race's outcome. Every dealing he had with the villain left him only more convinced that the man didn't love Verena.

To his regret, he had a feeling that was the way the lady preferred it.

"You show him, Shelburn," Lord Plunkett said from the sidelines. "I've got a monkey says you'll come in first."

Five hundred guineas said a lot for Plunkett's confidence that Shelburn would win. Eliot hoped to Hades that the man was mistaken.

"I appreciate your faith," Shelburn said before he glanced at Eliot. "I didn't anticipate quite this level of interest in our little contest, by Jupiter."

Eliot surveyed the heaving crowd. "Nor did I." He lowered his voice, although any chance for discretion had been lost the moment that he made his challenge, he feared. "Did you see Lady Verena last night?"

"I did. She's furious with me." Shelburn's lips curled in a wry smile. "Although given you started this whole thing, I got the impression that she's even more furious with you. If you see her in the next little while, I'd duck for cover, chum, or blood might be spilled. She's an excellent shot."

Eliot wasn't surprised to hear that Verena was fuming. She'd be even angrier than his dear papa. And that was saying something. In particular, she'd resent that he and Shelburn gambled with her fate, without giving her a say in what happened. Although he was bleakly aware that even if he banished

Shelburn from her side, society was full of men eager to share her bed.

"Are you ready, my lords?" Over the voice of the Angel's landlord, Eliot heard the town clock chiming eight. The din faded, as people realized that the race was about to start. "Clear the way. Clear the way. We don't want anyone hurt."

"I'm ready to show Lord Colville the way to Hatfield," Shelburn said with a self-assurance that made Eliot grind his teeth. When his hands tensed on the reins, the grays pricked their ears. He felt their quivering eagerness to be on the run.

Before Eliot could answer, the hum rose again to a new pitch of curiosity.

The crowd parted, not so that the race could begin, but to make room for a stylish cabriolet that bowled into the innyard at a dangerous pelt. "My lords, I believe I have a stake in this race."

It was Verena.

Of course it was. His heart rose at the sight of her. By God, he admired her spirit. This was no milk-and-water miss that he'd fallen in love with.

Eliot should have expected that she wouldn't be content to observe from a distance. He wondered whether she meant to cut up rough and try and stop the race. If she did, she'd left it deuced late to make her move.

"My lady, how pleasant to see you," Shelburn said, sweeping off his hat and giving her a deep bow from the seat of his carriage. "A fine Sunday morning for a rural frolic, wouldn't you say?"

Verena didn't smile, as Shelburn replaced his hat at a jaunty angle. She looked angry and determined, like Athena sweeping down from Olympus to restore law to disruptive humanity. All the military touches on her stylish red carriage dress only emphasized her martial air. She looked too beautiful for a man trying to come to terms with losing her forever.

"It's a fine Sunday morning for wanting to box the ears on a pair of presumptuous gentlemen. If scoundrels who toss a lady's name about in the public domain can even be called gentlemen."

The crowd watched in fascinated silence. As Eliot glanced around, he read avid enjoyment on every face. The race itself already promised splendid entertainment. Lady Verena's sudden arrival added extra spice to the diversion.

"Do you intend to join the race, my lady?" Shelburn asked, his voice light, as if no irate goddess blasted him with her fiery eyes.

"As a passenger only," she said, stepping down as her tiger ran forward to hold the horses.

"I'd be happy to take you up," Shelburn said, but she marched past him with a disdainful twitch of her hips.

"You can break your neck for all I care. I'll have a safer ride with Lord Colville."

An interested murmur rippled through the crowd, as Eliot stared at her in shock. "Are you saying you favor me to win, my lady?"

"I'm saying that I'm going to take my place at your side, because I refuse to see England's best hope of good governance crack his head open. Especially when he's on a misguided quest to show the world how dashing he is."

Lord Plunkett rushed forward to hand her up into Eliot's carriage. On the narrow seat, her hips wedged up against his in a most distracting fashion. As if sensing his disquiet, the grays shifted and pawed the ground.

"I don't give a rat's arse for the world, Verena," he said in an undertone. "I'm doing this for you."

Her lips took on an uncompromising line. "No, you're doing this for your own vanity."

The sharp response hardly registered. "You can't come with me, although I appreciate the show of support. I'll be too busy worrying about your safety to go all out to win."

She straightened her skirts and settled more firmly in the seat. "Precisely."

Blast it, all this wriggling made for more distraction. If she came with him, he feared that he'd land them both in the ditch through inattention to his driving. "I have to win."

"What if you do?" She shot him a furious glare. "This is a pudding-brained scheme. Even if you dismiss Shelburn as a rival, what happens next time I start a flirtation? You're going to beggar yourself at Tattersall's, buying horses to wager, my lord."

He shrugged. "You're worth any number of horses, Verena."

Eliot had hoped to make her smile, but she still looked like she wanted to give him a good hiding. "I'm past the stage where you can charm me. Right now, I'd like to shake you until your teeth rattle, you impulsive fool."

"Your fool," he said and turned his attention to the grays who were becoming edgy with the delay. "Always."

"Now we have a problem," Shelburn said. "You're carrying extra weight, Colville. I don't want anyone saying my victory wasn't won fair and square."

"Hardly gallant, Shelburn," Verena protested. "But if my participation makes the contest unequal, perhaps you should call it off."

He laughed again. Verena's intense displeasure seemed to amuse rather than dismay him. The devil must be cursed sure of her.

"No need." He surveyed the crowd, which seemed to have grown even larger than when Eliot came into the yard.

"You. The pretty miss in the blue dress over there." Shelburn pointed the handle of his whip at a group of people hovering on the edge of the throng. "Do you fancy a bit of excitement this morning? You look about Verena's size. What about a trip to Hatfield? I'll see you're escorted right and proper wherever you want to go afterward and throw a gold necklace into the mix to make it worth your while. What do you say? It will be a story you can tell the grandchildren over the fireside, when you're old and gray. The day you helped a rake win a race for another lady's heart."

Eliot waited for the woman to give Shelburn the set-down he deserved. No respectable female would take up such an offer. "I'll come with you, Shelburn," Lady Plunkett said from closer to the carriages.

Her husband guffawed and poked her in the ribs. "Emily, you're twice Verena's size. Don't be a nitwit."

Emily Plunkett, who was indeed rather plump, looked hurt as laughter echoed around the yard.

Eliot was astounded to see Shelburn's first choice step forward, to the clear displeasure of the soberly dressed man and woman beside her. "I'd be delighted to come, my lord."

"Kate, don't you dare," the woman behind her protested, but the attractive brunette ignored her. Instead, she marched forward and accepted Shelburn's hand, as he helped her up into his carriage.

"Good for you, miss," he said, giving her a lazy smile of appreciation.

Eliot glanced at Verena, who must resent the sight of her beau flirting with another woman. But she was watching Eliot rather than the other couple. "Call off this race, Eliot."

He gathered the ribbons in his gloved hands and gave her a brilliant smile. She might have rejected him in favor of Shelburn, but right now, she was with him. He intended to enjoy that, whatever happened next. "It's too late."

"Are you ready now, my lords?" the landlord asked. The stout fellow had climbed onto a wooden box so that everyone in the yard could see him.

"I am," Shelburn said.

His companion had settled next to him and regarded the crowd with a coolness that Eliot found remarkable. She looked as though playing a part in high-society antics was nothing out of the ordinary for her.

"Lord Colville?"

"Eager to go, landlord," he said.

Shelburn glanced across at him and touched the brim of his hat. For once, there was no derision in his dark eyes, and when he spoke, he sounded sincere as Eliot had never heard him before. "Good luck, Colville. May the best man win."

Before Eliot could come up with a suitably snide response, the landlord raised a large white handkerchief. "Make way. Make way. Good luck, my lords. Ready. Set. Go! And God save the King."

The man dropped the handkerchief. With a clatter of hooves and a rattle of wheels, the two carriages lurched into motion.

CHAPTER SEVENTEEN

o Eliot's relief, Verena remained silent while he negotiated the traffic outside the inn. As he'd said to her, her presence in his rig added an extra level of jeopardy to the race. When he'd made the challenge to Shelburn, he'd been in such a state of wild despair that he didn't much care if his recklessness ended in a broken neck. But be buggered if he was going to injure Verena.

The grays were fresh and skittish after the bedlam of the innyard. It took them a few minutes to find their rhythm, and Eliot needed all his skill to settle them into a fast gallop that would nonetheless keep them going until they reached Hatfield. All the noise and activity at the Angel had them ready to bolt.

Shelburn had made a better start than he had, damn the man's eyes. The chestnuts weren't as nervy as Eliot's horses, although he was convinced his were faster, if he could manage to bring the best out in them. He could no longer see his rival, who had bowled past just outside the Angel and had now disappeared ahead of a wagon piled high with old furniture.

Eliot stopped at the tollhouse at Highgate and flung some coins at the keeper. "Quick with the gate, man. Every second counts."

"Aye, my lord." The man touched his cap with respect before he dashed to open the gate. Eliot's payment had been well over the odds.

"There's a phaeton ahead of me. When did it come through?"

"A pair of fine chestnuts in harness and a pretty lady with the gentleman?"

"Yes, that's the one."

"He drove through about ten minutes ago. He was going at a goodly tilt."

That was what Eliot was afraid of, but he wasn't too discouraged. Ten minutes wasn't a lot of time to make up. "Thank you."

He urged the grays through the barrier and out onto the open road again. The horses gathered speed. They were brave creatures. He hoped to hell that he wouldn't be handing them over to Shelburn after he got to Hatfield.

When Verena spoke at last, to his surprise it wasn't with another scolding, but a compliment. They were out of the built-up area by then and fields stretched away on either side. Shelburn remained out of sight.

"That was sterling driving," she said.

He sent her a quick glance, before he returned his attention to the grays. They still showed signs of wanting to run until they stopped, which he feared would be well short of the twenty miles that they needed to cover. "Thank you."

"I thought that stagecoach was going to hit us when the road narrowed, but you went past as sweet as sugar. Even if you lose today, your reputation as a whip will be assured."

Eliot's lips flattened. "I have no intention of losing."

"Shelburn's well ahead."

"There's still a long way to go," he said, even as he clicked his teeth at the grays to go faster. At last, they were running as smooth as silk and for the moment, the road ahead was clear and straight.

"Yes, there is," she said in a musing tone that made him wonder if she was talking about more than just the horse race.

"You don't sound as angry as you did."

Verena sighed. She was near enough for him to feel her ribs expand under the close-fitting red spencer. "Last night when I heard about this ridiculous display, I wanted to flay you alive."

"I don't doubt that." Sardonic amusement lifted the corners of his lips. "You still looked ready to commit murder this morning, when you descended on the Angel like a vengeful fury. I'm just grateful you weren't carrying your pistols."

She didn't smile, but she didn't sound as if she was furious with him anymore either, thank heaven. For the life of him, he couldn't pinpoint her mood at all. Which was odd in itself, because he'd spent most of the last year finely tuned to the state of Verena's emotions.

"With both of you acting like children, perhaps a spanking would do more good than a bullet."

"That's never been my vice, although I gather Lord Brice pays a maid to give him a good thrashing with a wooden paddle before he can perform with his wife."

That earned him a startled glance and distracted her from giving him a lecture. Which had been his plan. "I hadn't heard that."

"You'd be surprised what men talk about when it's late at night and we're waiting for a parliamentary division."

His colleagues had gossiped about Verena, too, in terms that now made him livid. It wasn't much consolation now to remember that at the time, saintly Lord Colville hadn't joined in, even if he couldn't avoid listening. The woman he'd come to know bore no resemblance to the rapacious hussy in those salacious tales.

They clattered through a village where a Sunday service must have just ended. A crowd of people gathered outside the church.

Without warning, a child of about five darted out in front of the carriage. While Verena gasped in horror, Eliot managed to avoid a collision. With a scream, the little boy's mother rushed up to haul her son to safety.

As Eliot gave an apologetic wave and urged the grays on, the congregation leveled a battery of disapproving stares at him. Today saintly Lord Colville was far from the usual model of propriety.

By all that was holy, he was sick to the back teeth of being saintly Viscount Colville. Whatever happened between him and Verena – and her attitude this morning wasn't nearly as forbidding as he'd feared it might be – at least that was one weight off his shoulders.

In truth, he'd never much liked his righteous reputation. He'd always been too aware of his many flaws. Those flaws had become even more obvious over recent weeks. No saint would compete in a horse race on the Lord's Day. No saint would harbor the violent dislike that he'd developed for Shelburn. No saint would want to fuck Verena until he couldn't remember his own name.

"Get on!" he shouted at his grays, and the valiant beasts boosted their speed as they approached the next hill.

From the top, Eliot saw that Shelburn's elegant carriage was only about half a mile ahead. The sight cheered him immeasurably. His horses were going well and still had plenty of pepper in them, whereas even from this distance, he could see that Shelburn's cattle were laboring. That fast start from Islington was costing him now.

"I can look after the toll at Barnet," Verena said. "It will be quicker, if you don't have to fiddle around looking for money."

A wry smile quirked his lips. "Careful, Verena, that sounds like you want me to win."

She didn't look at him, and he still couldn't judge her mood from her enigmatic profile. When she'd climbed into the carriage, he'd braced to receive the sharp side of her tongue all the way to Hatfield. Or perhaps for her to sulk for the whole twenty miles.

It hadn't turned out that way. She was quieter than usual, but she wasn't seething with resentment.

"I'd hate you to lose these horses. They're magnificent."

He didn't comment on the fact that if he won, she lost her chance with Shelburn. Her partisanship on his behalf made frail hope stir in his heart.

"In that case, thank you," he said, transferring the reins to one hand to dig his coin purse from his coat pocket. "I'd appreciate you taking over the toll payments."

She accepted the purse and set it in her lap. A thin leather strap held her stylish hat in place, and a few strands of hair whipped around her face. One red-gloved hand curved around the rail at the end of the seat, but the furious pace didn't appear to daunt her.

How vividly alive she looked. She always did.

Verena was a woman who fed on excitement. She mightn't approve of the motives behind the race, but this brisk run on a sunny spring morning would stir her blood. Perhaps that was why she was in a better mood than he'd anticipated. It was possible that her attitude toward Eliot hadn't softened at all.

"Hold on. This is a good spot to pass Shelburn without putting anyone in danger."

She firmed her grip on the rail and lifted her other hand to hold her hat. "Good luck, Eliot."

"What the devil…"

"Watch the road, you lunatic. We're going too fast for you to get distracted."

That fragile tendril of hope stretched toward the sun. No question, she was on his side.

But as she said, now was no time for a heart-to-heart. It would be just his luck if Verena decided that she could stomach him as a suitor, just before he landed them both in the gravel.

He shifted his grip on the ribbons and urged the grays on. They responded like the champions they were. The carriage bounced along the road at a snapping pace. With every minute, the distance narrowed between him and Shelburn.

"Are you all right?" he shouted at Verena. The wind whistled past so fast, he had to speak up to make sure she heard him.

"Marvelous," she said.

Despite their speed, he checked to see if she was being sarcastic. But her lovely face was flushed with elation, and her eyes sparkled with the thrill of the contest.

As the grays galloped up behind them, Shelburn and his companion – Kate? – turned.

Shelburn encouraged his chestnuts to go faster, but his lead was decreasing. Within minutes, Eliot was right beside him.

Shelburn flashed him a smile that expressed the same exhilaration Eliot felt. "I see you've woken up, Colville," he called across the tiny gap between the two carriages. "About time."

The woman at his side should look terrified. But as she watched Eliot pass them, her face was eager. Egad, she was as cool a customer as Verena, it seemed. Shelburn had made a lucky guess when he'd chosen her. Most of the ladies of Eliot's acquaintance would have fits of the vapors if he drove them at half this rate.

"Just lulling you into a false sense of security, old man," Eliot said breathlessly, giving the grays their heads. By now, both carriages were flying ahead at a mad pace.

The chestnuts were intrepid gallopers, but Eliot had been right to judge his cattle as swifter. Slowly but surely, the grays outpaced their competition. Then they were past, and the empty road extended ahead.

"Well done, Eliot," Verena said, her voice vibrating with excitement. "You've got him at a disadvantage now."

"I intend to keep him that way, too."

Eliot waited until the curricle had pulled a safe distance in front, before he angled it back onto the right side of the road. They didn't have far to go to reach the Barnet tollgate. That meant that they were more than halfway to Hatfield, and he meant to lead the way until the end.

They climbed another hill. When he checked back, Shelburn fell even further behind. The chestnuts were fine horses, but the combination of the grays' fleetness and Eliot's desperation was proving to make him unbeatable.

They clattered through the Barnet tollgate with barely a minute's delay to pay the keeper. Then they were back on the road, with less than nine miles to go.

"Verena..."

"Don't talk now." She tucked her arm into his side and snuggled closer. Despite the day's myriad excitements, that was the most exciting thing that had happened since they'd set out. "You've got a race to win."

"I have, haven't I?" Although he'd already built up a substantial lead, he encouraged the grays to a swifter pace.

Eliot had another reason now for making the best time he could. When they reached Hatfield, he had things to say to Verena. He wondered if perhaps at last, she might be ready to hear him.

Caution still lingered. He couldn't forget the night that she'd taken him to her bed in London, when he thought all his dreams had come true. Instead, he'd come crashing down to earth and the realization that nothing had changed since her emphatic rejection of his proposal.

The sun grew warmer. Around them, the hedgerows and the verges of the road were bright with wildflowers. Spring had arrived in all its beauty. This was the first day that Eliot had been in a frame of mind to appreciate it.

The black and white dog appeared out of nowhere. It streaked across the road just under the horse's noses.

The grays neighed wildly and veered hard to the side. With a lurch, the left wheel sank deep into the soft grass on the verge, and the carriage scraped the blackthorn hedge.

"Hell's bells!" Eliot gasped. He battled to get his horses under control. "For God's sake, hold on, Verena."

The grays plunged in the traces and wrenched hard against his desperate grip. With all his strength, he fought to bring them back into line. They were within a whisker of bolting. If they did, he feared that the curricle would end up in splinters and heaven knew if he'd be able to save Verena.

Despite his best efforts, he felt the carriage tipping. He'd lay money that they were about to go over.

He leaned his weight in the other direction and without his asking, Verena leaned into him. She was soft and warm and shaking with terror, and he'd willingly forego touching her ever again, if he could just keep her safe and get her out of this mess.

"Steady, there. Steady there, boys." Despite his panic, he kept his voice low and soothing. "It's all right. Nothing to worry about."

As he kept up the calming litany, the carriage bounced back on two wheels with a shudder and a loud creak. The horses were still upset, but at least Eliot had them under control. He doubted that they'd try and make a run for it now, although if anything else popped out to startle them, they'd be off like a shot.

He sucked in his first proper breath since the dog's appearance. Dazed eyes took in his surroundings. The day was still clear and warm, despite death brushing past, closer than he'd driven alongside Shelburn's phaeton back before Barnet.

"Can you sit up on your own, Verena? I'd help you, but I don't want to let the ribbons go."

"Dear Lord above, haven't you already given me enough excitement for the morning?" she gasped, struggling back to her corner of the seat. She'd lost her hat, and her lovely hair tumbled about her face in beguiling disarray.

"Are you all right?"

"A few bruises, I think, but nothing a glass of brandy won't help."

Eliot made himself laugh, more as a tribute to her spirit than because he was genuinely amused. By heaven, she was a champ. "I'll send you a case when I get back to London."

"Make it two." She tried to sound like her usual ironic, collected self, but didn't quite succeed.

With every minute, the grays became quieter. The dog had disappeared through a gap in the thicket and was nowhere to be seen. At last, Eliot's pulse started to revert to its normal speed.

"You're on." He turned to face her. Verena was pale, and her blue eyes were dark with the remnants of fear. "Will you take the reins, while I get down and check the horses and the rig? I want to be sure we're safe to go on."

"Of course."

Eliot passed her the ribbons and climbed down, ashamed of how his legs quivered with reaction. He kept reliving that moment when the world had threatened to turn upside down and transform everything to catastrophe.

After hefting in another tattered breath, he made himself walk up to take the horses' heads. The poor, frightened beasts were blowing and shivering. Sheets of sweat covered their glossy withers.

"Shh, Mick, it's all right, old man. It's all right. That nasty dog has gone. You're safe. You're such a good fellow. Such a good, grand, brave fellow."

Mick, whose full name was the Archangel Michael of Tipton, and his brother Bob, properly Robert the Bruce of Tipton, soon lowered their heads under the low, comforting crooning. The prosaic names that his grooms used for his thoroughbreds usually amused Eliot. Not today. He wasn't yet in any state to smile at anything.

He, Mick and Bob could all be dead by the side of the road. Even worse, so could Verena. Nausea clawed at his heaving gut as he imagined all her fire and intelligence and beauty coming to destruction.

He kept murmuring to the horses and stroking their necks and quivering flanks, until he was sure that they were over their fright. Only then did he dare to leave them to walk back to where Verena sat in the curricle, clutching the ribbons.

"Mick and Bob?" She sounded like her usual self. She'd recovered her composure with impressive swiftness.

"It's less of a mouthful than their full names."

"I like it."

Eliot reached into his coat and produced a flat silver flask. He unscrewed the lid and passed it to her. "Here's my lady's brandy."

"Thank you." She transferred the reins to one hand and took a generous swig. "That's better."

When she returned the flask, he was pleased to see a hint of color in her face. Aware that his lips touched the same place that hers had, he took a mouthful of the spirits, too.

He replaced the stopper and handed the flask back to Verena. "Just in case you need some more."

The liquor helped to steady his still-leaping nerves. He couldn't help thinking about what might have happened just now, if luck hadn't been on their side. "There's a basket under the seat. I brought some apples. I think the boys deserve a small treat."

"So do I." Verena set the flask on the seat beside her and leaned down to pull out the large wicker basket.

He opened the lid. After a rummage, he found a couple of apples and a knife. "There's bread and cheese in there, if you're hungry."

Her wry laugh reassured him that she was going to be fine. He wasn't so sure that he was. "I'm not ready for food yet. If you hadn't been so brilliant with the horses, I've got a feeling I'd be smashed to pieces in a hedgerow."

He had the same feeling, and it made him feel sick. Because it was all his fault that she'd been in danger in the first place.

"We were lucky," he said with a hint of abruptness, before he headed up to give the horses their treat. He couldn't force any more words through the great logjam of emotion blocking his throat.

Bob was nosing at the grass at the roadside, and Mick looked uncharacteristically docile with his head down and one front leg bent in a relaxed pose. They'd recovered from their shock faster than he had.

Eliot took his time with them, praising them and scratching behind their ears and feeding them the apples in chunks. When they were over their scare enough to nudge him in equine greed, he left them to give the curricle a thorough check for cracks. Everything seemed in good shape, which was almost unbelievable, considering the speed that he'd been going when he came off the road.

Once he was sure that the rig was safe, he bent to untangle Verena's hat from the bushes. As he passed it up to her, he noticed that the strap was broken. "I'm not sure it's still wearable."

With a shrug, she accepted it. "Better my hat takes a battering then we do."

She tugged the last of the pins from her hair. The carriage ensemble featured a white cravat like a man's. With a couple of efficient movements, she unwound it and tied her hair back from her face.

"Very becoming," he said, trying to summon a smile. He bent to pick up the coin purse and slip it into his pocket. When the carriage lurched to the side, it had fallen to the ground.

"I'll arrive in Hatfield looking like a milkmaid, but if you don't mind that, I don't."

"I don't mind," he said, his tone flat enough to earn him a curious glance. To his relief, she didn't question his lackluster response.

Eliot climbed up beside Verena and set the grays off at a gentle amble. He was grateful that it was a sleepy Sunday morning and no traffic came past to unnerve his horses again.

She passed the flask back. He took another sip, but nothing could banish the sour feeling lodged in the pit of his stomach. He put away the brandy and stared blindly past the grays' ears to the road unwinding ahead.

After about five minutes of modest progress, Verena spoke. "Eliot, don't you think you should get them going again? I know you've got a good lead over Shelburn, but there's still a couple of miles to Hatfield. You don't want him to catch up. It is a race, after all."

Instead of heeding her suggestion, he drew the horses to a stop. With shaking hands, he tied the reins to the front rail. The grays wouldn't bolt again now, although they wouldn't appreciate another delay. He'd felt how eager they were to pick up the pace.

In preparation for the difficult moments to come, he squared his jaw. Admitting that one had been criminally misguided was never easy. Failure tasted rank on his tongue and settled in a great acrid weight in his gut. "I don't give a rat's arse about the race anymore."

Her jaw dropped in shock, and she regarded him in baffled dismay. "I don't understand."

Eliot swallowed to clear his throat before he spoke in an urgent rush, his voice harsh with the intensity of his emotions. "I've been wrong, Verena. Wrong about so much. I won't ask you to forgive me, because I'll never forgive myself."

Somewhere during those frantic minutes of almost crashing his carriage, Eliot's conscience had awoken from its temporary slumber. Now it was hurling recriminations at him fit to make his head ring.

Eliot was a man of powerful conscience. During most of his life, he'd followed its dictates. For God's sake, only his conscience had prevented him from breaking with his pig of a father years ago. It insisted that he owed a duty to Imogen and the title and the people on the estate.

Over the last few weeks, his turbulent feelings for Verena had drowned out the sensible inner voice that told him what was right and wrong. But the near disaster on the road had knocked him back to reality with a painful jolt. Now the cold eye of reason surveyed his behavior, and he was appalled at what he saw.

He'd been acting like a barbarian. Worse, he'd been acting like a fool.

"I wasn't injured," Verena said in a matter-of-fact voice.

A humorless smile curved his mouth. "Praise heaven, you weren't. But you shouldn't have been in this carriage. You wouldn't have been, if I'd kept my bloody trap shut. I shouldn't have challenged Shelburn. I have no claim on you. I have no license to interfere in your life. I have no right to chase away any man you fancy. I've been behaving like a selfish brute." Then the worst admission of all. "I've been behaving like my father."

"That's not true," Verena said, but reality was too stark for him to find any comfort in her assurances.

"I love you, Verena, but I don't own you. Dear God, one of the things I love most about you is that you're such a law unto yourself."

"You'd be alone there," she said with a hint of bitterness.

It was his turn to shrug. "Then I'm alone. But I've always thought your independence was brave and true. I still think that, even though I've spent the last few weeks trying to bend you to my will."

Eliot swallowed again to ease his constricted throat. He owed her this apology, but that didn't make it any easier. He continued in a low voice that vibrated with sincerity. "I won't act the petty tyrant anymore, Verena. You're free of me. You're free to take any lover you choose. You're free to forget me. In fact, you're just free. I'll never trouble you again."

CHAPTER EIGHTEEN

Verena surveyed Eliot in mounting horror, while every word she'd told him that she wanted to hear followed on from the last. Her trembling hands twined in her lap as acid tears stung her eyes, blurring her view. Although not enough to allow her to pretend that he didn't mean what he said. Or to conceal just how beautiful he was.

He'd never looked more like a valiant knight of old. His jaw was hard and determined. His expressive mouth was stern. His gray eyes were steady. Only the muscle flickering in his cheek betrayed what it cost him to let her go.

"But, Eliot, what if I don't want you to set me free?" Her voice emerged as a shaky whisper.

When he didn't immediately respond, she wondered if he'd heard, although he sat mere inches away.

After a few seconds, she saw his Adam's apple move as he swallowed. His eyes grew intent. "Just what are you saying, Verena?"

This time, he wasn't going to accept anything but unconditional surrender. She couldn't blame him. She'd hurt him so deeply, although that had never been her purpose. Not only that, but she'd tainted his standing in the world. After today, there would be even more nasty talk. Loving her had destroyed his good name.

But while she felt guilty about how she'd tormented him and she regretted turning him into a figure almost as scandalous as she was, she wasn't sorry that they'd reached this point. Because a night of uncomfortable soul-searching had revealed that she didn't give a fig for what the world said. She never had.

At last, she was ready to break free of the prison that had held her captive since her disastrous marriage. Now that she'd stared death square in his cold, cold eyes, her decision to marry Eliot seemed even more urgent. She had one life. She had no intentions now of spending it without him.

Verena struggled to give him a smile but couldn't quite manage it. No matter how she tried, she couldn't stop her voice from trembling either. "I'm saying, my darling saintly Lord Colville, that if you're still willing to take me as your wife, I'm most willing to be taken."

The vulnerability in his expression threatened to break her heart. She saw how much he wanted to believe her, but couldn't quite allow himself to.

"Verena…" He reached out and caught her arms in desperate hands. "Have you stopped running at last?"

Curse these tears. And the stupid thing was that she was happy. Why the devil was she crying?

She blinked to clear her vision, but it remained misty. "I'll always run to you, my love."

His hands tightened. Even through the fine wool of her spencer, the heat of his touch stirred her blood. "But you were so angry this morning when you arrived at the inn."

A tremulous smile greeted that. "You were making yourself an object of ridicule."

"You know why I did it."

"Yes, to show me that you don't care about scandal."

"That's true." He sent her a rueful look. "But mainly it was to keep you away from Shelburn. I've been trapped in a hell of jealousy since you sent me away. I'm not proud of myself."

Once, she might have resented that hint of ownership. She would with any other man. But she couldn't bear to picture Eliot marrying someone else, so she was in no position to feel superior.

"My dear, no man has touched me since the day we came together. No other man will." She reached up to shape a hand to the angle of that princely jaw. Her voice thickened with emotion. "That is if you'll have me. You haven't answered me yet, you know."

"I'll have you every day of the week, you wonderful girl." He pressed his face into her hand, and his smile broadened. "I was yours from the first. Now I think that perhaps you might have decided to be mine."

"Yes, I'm yours, Eliot. There's no perhaps about it. I can't resist you." Tears started to trickle down her face. "I love you. So very much."

She'd admitted that she loved him once before, but it had been a grudging confession and the prelude to rejecting him. Now she spoke the words with all the adoration filling her heart.

She'd imagined that it might be difficult to promise herself to a man ever again. But with this man, it felt like a new kind of freedom. The vow emerged as naturally as water flowed downhill to the sea. So easy that she said the words again just for sheer pleasure. "I love you, Eliot."

Verena saw his face change, as at last he realized that she yielded to her love and that she entrusted herself to him forever. He leaned forward and kissed her softly on the lips, as if she was fragile and sweet and innocent. As if she was the girl that she'd been before those dark years with George.

Something in that reverent, tender kiss restored her lost innocence. She kissed him back with a trace of shyness that she knew he sensed, because his touch turned even gentler and his lips conveyed worship instead of passion.

By the time he raised his head, she felt made anew. She would come to Eliot, worthy to be his bride. It didn't matter what the world might say about her. She and her beloved knew the truth about the purity of the love that united them.

"I love you, too, Verena. I've loved you from the first. What changed for you? I was so sure I'd lost you forever."

"You were right. I was frightened." As her thirsty heart opened wide to take in his declaration, her lips turned down in self-disgust. "But I'm not frightened anymore. You're the best thing that ever happened to me, yet I was letting the shadows of the past steal away all hope of happiness. Will you forgive me for hurting you?"

He leaned in and kissed her with more heat. By the time they drew apart, they were both trembling with the power of the emotions surging between them. "Right now, I'm so happy I could forgive Lucifer himself."

She managed a broken laugh. "I'm wicked, but I'm not quite as bad as that."

Eliot stared at her as if she was the sun that warmed his days to light. She swore then and there that she'd do her best to make sure he always looked at her that way.

The carriage creaked as Mick moved in the traces. They probably shouldn't leave the horses standing too long, but Verena couldn't bear to bring this radiant moment to an end. Not just yet.

Eliot cupped her cheek in one hand and brushed his thumb over the trails of her drying tears. "I hope that you'll still be wicked with me."

She reached up to give him a quick kiss. "Only with you, my beloved."

"Only with me."

This time, he lashed his arms around her and drew her as close as the narrow carriage seat allowed. His lips explored hers with silent promises of love and faith and protection. Promises that he'd speak in front of a vicar before the next few days were out. Promises that would bind them together for eternity.

Once that prospect would have terrified Verena into a gibbering mess. Now she couldn't wait. She kissed him back, making her own silent vows of everlasting allegiance.

"About time," a mocking voice drawled from behind them. Verena had been so wrapped up in the man she loved that she hadn't heard Shelburn's carriage approach.

Eliot raised his head without any particular rush. He kept his arm around Verena, as the phaeton rolled to a stop beside them. "I see you've caught up at last, Shelburn," he said with commendable coolness. "You can be the first to congratulate us. Lady Verena has just agreed to marry me."

"It seems she's made her choice." Shelburn was kind enough to pretend regret. "I bow to the better man."

Verena really did have a good friend in him. When she'd heard about the race, she'd been puzzled as well as angry that he wagered something he didn't value against Eliot's marvelous horses. But now she wondered if perhaps he'd hoped that the race would bring her romance with Eliot to a happy conclusion.

"Thank you." Eliot's grip firmed on her. "I'd offer my condolences, but as you're about to win the race, you'll have my grays. That should console you."

Shelburn gave a dismissive wave. "Keep them as an early wedding present. In my view, the race has ended in a draw. Or, no, not quite. You've come out the winner in the only way that counts."

"Perhaps you should introduce us to your companion." Verena glanced at the woman beside Shelburn, who observed them with intelligent hazel eyes. "I assume that somewhere over the last fifteen miles, you've managed to exchange names."

Shelburn cast the dark-haired woman an unreadable glance. Verena recognized sexual interest, but that was no surprise. He was a rake, after all. But there was something new in his expression that she couldn't quite identify. "Lady Verena Gerard, Lord Colville. Allow me to present Miss Catherine Starr of Bradbourne in Derbyshire."

Eliot bent his head. "Miss Starr."

Verena smiled. Right now, she wanted to smile at the whole world. "Miss Starr."

The woman smiled back. She was a handsome creature. "My lady. My lord. May I add my congratulations into the mix?"

"You may," Verena said.

"Go ahead and claim the victory, my lord," Eliot said. "We had a bit of a mishap with the curricle about a mile back. It seems to be in one piece, but I don't want to take too many chances with my precious cargo."

Shelburn frowned. "What the devil happened?"

"A dog ran out in front of us and nearly brought us to grief," Verena said. "No real harm was done."

In fact, much good had come out of that reckless hound's perilous dash. She'd intended to make everything right with Eliot when they reached Hatfield and he no longer had to worry about controlling his team. But the sweetness of exchanging their vows of love in this lush countryside setting would always be a cherished memory.

"Thank the Lord for that." Shelburn turned to Eliot. "If you can bear to share a carriage, Colville, you and I could come in together in my rig and officially make it a draw. That way, the people who placed wagers will get to keep their blunt."

Verena considered this option and dismissed it. "If Eliot arrives at Hatfield as your passenger, people will still say you won because it's your carriage. I've got a better idea. My cabriolet is coming up behind us. With the delays, I imagine it will show up any minute."

Actually, now that she thought a little more about delays, she was surprised at how far Shelburn had been behind them. He should have been closer on their heels, if he was pushing his team hard enough to win the race.

Her questioning gaze dwelled on his face, but he was busy looking interested and pleased at the news of her engagement. That convinced her even more that he'd done his best to ensure that Eliot came in first.

When she caught his eye, his innocent air only confirmed her suspicions. She sent him a small, grateful smile and went on with what she meant to suggest. "Why don't you two gentlemen travel in my rig with my horses? Miss Starr and I can follow in

Shelburn's phaeton with the grays, and my groom can bring the curricle in last with the chestnuts. I wouldn't leave the grays to him. He's got a good pair of hands, but the horses have had a fright and need careful handling. That is if you'll trust the grays to me, darling?"

Eliot smiled at her with more of that unabashed adoration. Warmth filled her, a warmth that she knew would remain with her for the rest of her days. "I trust you with my life. And my horses."

She laughed, even as she sent him an equally besotted look. "I promise on my soul to take good care of both." She turned back to Shelburn, who was looking rather abashed at the conversation's sentimental turn. "What do you think? Miss Starr, I'm a good driver, if you're nervous at all. Or if you're unsure, you can travel with my groom. In any case, it's only a couple of miles."

"I'm sure you're more than competent, my lady," Miss Starr replied with what appeared to be her usual aplomb. "I'd be honored to be your passenger."

Verena was curious about this woman who had so readily accepted Shelburn's invitation. She looked like a respectable citizen. Her dark blue traveling ensemble was in the first stare of fashion, and the blue-blooded company didn't appear to overawe her.

There was some mystery here, Verena was sure. Perhaps she'd discover it on the way to Hatfield.

"That's a capital solution," Shelburn said. "Given the race has ended with a joyous result but no genuine victor, this should satisfy all parties."

Eliot climbed down and stared up at Verena with his heart in his silvery eyes. He'd been staring at her with his heart in his eyes for nearly a year, but she'd been too lost in old miseries to realize it.

"I hate to let you go, now that I've got you to consent to marrying me." He spoke in a low tone, so only she could hear. "I want to laugh and talk and plan. Not to mention, I want to kiss you and hold you close and spend hours wondering at how well everything has turned out."

Tenderness flooded her, as she gazed down into that remarkable face. "I hate to leave you, too, but we've got the rest of our lives to congratulate ourselves on our excellent judgement in deciding to marry."

He laughed, then looked behind him. "Your rig is coming up the road right now."

She glanced back and saw Smith approaching at a measured pace. "Let's put the race behind us, then we can concentrate on just the two of us."

"If I get a special license tomorrow, will you marry me this week? Or we could call the banns at St. George's and make our vows in a couple of weeks under society's full glare."

She smiled down at him, enchanted anew. So many times, he'd told her that he was proud of her. His willingness to wed her in front of the world and his wife just confirmed it. "I had a big wedding first time around, and it was a catastrophe from the beginning. Let's do something small for us, then have a long honeymoon."

His smile developed a devilish edge that suited him surprisingly well. "No wonder I love you."

"I'm very glad you do." Her mind focused on the forthcoming wedding. "Let's do the pretty in a week. I want a couple of days to have a new dress made. I'd like to look my best when I pledge my life and heart to you."

"I wouldn't have it any other way." While Shelburn and Verena's groom started on the changes to the horses, Colville crossed to the phaeton and held one hand out to Shelburn's passenger. "May I assist you out of the carriage while we swap the teams over, Miss Starr? Lady Verena has a wonderful touch with the ribbons. You couldn't be in safer hands."

"Thank you." She lightly stepped down.

Within ten minutes, the new arrangements were in place. As he urged her horses to a run, Eliot blew Verena a kiss whose mocking edge in no way lessened his fervent message of love. His rival sat beside him in apparent ease.

Verena urged the grays to follow at a gentler rate. Miss Starr maintained the calmness that seemed to be her habit. Smith had taken charge of the damaged curricle and brought up the rear.

The imprudent race to Hatfield had reached an unexpected, but perfect denouement. Verena knew that she and Eliot had found the perfect ending to their clandestine love affair as well. The love would go on forever. The affair would turn into a lifetime of passionate joy for the angelic Lord Colville and his audacious lady.

EPILOGUE

Trentham Hall, Wiltshire, May 1818

Verena kissed Eliot with deep, succulent carnality and rose over him on her knees. Steaming water sloshed against the marble sides of the huge tub. It held pride of place in the bathing chamber that now adjoined the viscount's apartments in his gracious Elizabethan manor house. Originally this room had been assigned to the viscountess but, as Verena pointed out, she only ever slept in Eliot's bed anyway.

As he fondled her wet breasts, she straddled him and sank down to take him into her body. Even after almost two years of marriage, the immediacy of the pleasure shocked her. He filled all of her, body and soul. She gazed into his eyes, reading hunger and enjoyment and best of all, invincible, eternal love.

"Ah, yes," he sighed, leaning his head back against the edge of the bath and tilting his hips to thrust deeper.

She tensed around him and watched heat flare in those velvety gray eyes. The soft afternoon light through the open casement windows shone gold on his chiseled features. He still looked like Sir Galahad. He still surprised her with daring sensual adventures that no pure and holy knight would think to attempt.

"How is it that this is always new?" she murmured, leaning forward to press her breasts deeper into his palms. He tugged at her nipples just the way she liked it, almost to the point of discomfort. Every pinch of those long fingers on the sensitive tips sent a bolt of sensation sizzling to her womb. When she shifted experimentally, the pressure inside her altered in a most exquisite fashion.

"That's easy to answer," he said, his joy in her unhidden. An enchanted smile stretched his lips. He bumped upward again as she circled her hips, taking her time. "It's love, Verena. Love alone has this magic. I love you more now than I did when I married you. And then I loved you so much that every beat of my heart spoke your name."

"Oh, Eliot," she whispered and leaned down to kiss him again. "You're such a romantic."

"Am I wrong?"

"No, you're not." She rose with a voluptuous slowness that had him gasping before she lowered again. Once again, she yielded to the transcendent connection. "I'm so glad you didn't let me get away."

With languorous appreciation, he combed his hands through the veils of rich brown hair clinging to her slippery skin. "I'm so glad you let me catch you."

Verena suspected that her smile was as besotted as his. "We were lucky, weren't we?"

"So lucky." He brought her down for another kiss. When he pulled away, she was trembling.

"Now take your pleasure, my darling." His soft baritone vibrated with anticipation. "I'm at your service."

She set her hands flat on his chest and began to move, swift to find her rhythm and succumb to the familiar rise of ecstasy. Soon she was undulating in a wild ride, sending water spilling over the sides of the bath.

With a groan, Eliot gripped her hips and brought her down hard when she crashed through into hot, quaking bliss. As she cried out at her peak, she felt him flood her with his seed.

Still shaking, she collapsed over him, gasping in the thick, humid air. His arms curled around her, holding her against his pounding heart.

For a long while, she lay upon him, breathless after the rapturous journey that they'd just taken. She loved the peace that filled her soul after she and Eliot climbed to heaven. Until she'd married him, peace had been a stranger in her life. Its sweetness added a glow to everything that they did together.

A tired but exultant smile curved her lips, as she thought back over the last two eventful years. There had been so many changes, not least in the restless, brittle widow who once strove to fill an empty life with constant activity. She'd feared marriage for so long, but it turned out to be the best thing that she'd ever done. The Verena who lay in Eliot's arms now was gentler and kinder and more self-aware than the brazen lady who had set the beau monde on its ear.

A week after that dramatic carriage race to Hatfield, she and Eliot had married in a quiet ceremony at St. James in Piccadilly. None of his family had attended. Stella and Halston had been on their honeymoon. Imogen was exiled to Gloucestershire. After Eliot placed the notice of their forthcoming marriage in the *Morning Post*, his father had publicly disowned him.

To nobody's surprise, the storm of gossip raging around the unlikely union between the sinner and the saint had been vociferous and cruel. But by then, Verena had had enough of high society and its hypocrisies. After a glorious wedding trip to Paris, she and Eliot had retired to his estate in Wiltshire and established a fulfilling, busy, useful life.

At the next election, Eliot had left parliament to concentrate on local issues. Here in Wiltshire, he was an active justice of the peace and he'd done wonders with the estate, developing it into a model of modern farming practices.

Now that he was famous for his agricultural innovations, landowners came from far and wide to seek his advice. And Verena's. To her surprise, it turned out that all those centuries of land management running through her bloodlines meant that she'd taken to country life as if born to it.

Sometimes she met her eyes in the mirror and wondered how flighty, unhappy Verena Gerard had become this contented, purposeful creature.

Eliot was right. The transformation was all down to love

"I'm glad we had the floor tiled," Eliot murmured with lazy amusement, as he stroked her glistening flank. "Carpet or wooden boards wouldn't cope with the flood we cause every time we bathe together."

With a weary laugh, she rubbed her cheek against his shoulder. There was a spot between his neck and shoulder that was specifically created for her to rest her head against. A perfect fit. But then, everything about Eliot was a perfect fit for her.

Who would have thought that the wickedest woman in London and virtuous Lord Colville should turn out to be exactly right for each other?

"You put such thought into our bathing chamber. I'm in awe at your cleverness. The steam-powered pulleys from the kitchen, so the poor servants don't break their backs carrying water up all those stairs? Genius. And the way the pipes take away the waste water? Even smarter." She paused. "I'm hoping you can perform similar magic in the nursery."

A charged silence descended. Eliot's body turned rigid beneath hers, and his caressing hand went still. "Verena, have you got something to tell me?"

She sat up slowly. When she shared the secret that she'd carried for the last two months, she wanted to look into his eyes. She'd so hungered to give him a child. At first, she'd feared that only wishful thinking led her to imagine she was pregnant. "I'm going to have a baby, Eliot. Around Christmas, I think."

Incandescent joy lit his face and he sat up, too, splashing more water onto the floor. He caught her shoulders and stared at her as if she brought the stars down from the sky and set them in his lap for his delight. "My darling, you make me so happy."

She blinked back silly tears. "I wanted to be sure before I told you. I was so convinced that this would never happen."

"How are you feeling?"

"Marvelous." She gave him a beaming smile, even if one that was a little misty around the edges. "Like I want to take on the world. I thought I'd be sick and miserable, but all I want to do is eat. I suspect by the time the baby comes, I'll be the size of an elephant."

When he grinned back, she'd never seen a man look more elated. "I'll have a lovely, plump little wife to fuss over. I can't wait."

"Soon none of my old clothes will fit me." Life in the country hadn't lessened her interest in fashion. "I'll need a new wardrobe."

Eliot rolled his eyes in fond mockery. "Of course you will."

She drew one of his hands across to rest on her bare stomach, which as yet showed no sign of the life growing within. "You can't expect your son to put up with a frump for a mother."

"I want my daughter to grow up as dashing and stylish as her mamma." He curled his fingers against her skin in a tender gesture of protection. When his voice lowered, she caught a hint of the powerful emotion flowing beneath his teasing. "I love you so much, my darling. Thank you for marrying me. I already knew that I was the happiest man in England. Now the arrival of a baby as the fruit of our love is almost too much to comprehend."

Drat these tears. She sniffed and gave him another watery but jubilant smile. "And I love you."

In a silent gesture of adoration, Eliot laced his fingers through hers. "Kiss me, Verena."

"With pleasure, my beloved husband." Verena leaned forward and whispered a promise against his parted lips. "Always with pleasure. Always with love."

ABOUT THE AUTHOR

Australian Anna Campbell has written 11 multi award-winning historical romances for Avon HarperCollins and Grand Central Publishing. As an independently published author, she's released more than 30 bestselling stories. Right now, she is working on a new series called Scoundrels of Mayfair, set amidst the glamour and sensuality of Regency London. Anna has won numerous awards for her stories, including RT Book Reviews Reviewers Choice, the Booksellers Best, the Golden Quill (three times), the Heart of Excellence (twice), the Write Touch, the Aspen Gold (twice), and the Australian Romance Readers' favorite historical romance (five times).

Anna loves to hear from her readers. You can find her at:

Website: www.annacampbell.com

facebook.com/AnnaCampbellFans

twitter.comAnnaCampbellOz

bookbub.com/authors/anna-campbell

One Wicked Wish:
A Scandal in Mayfair Book 1

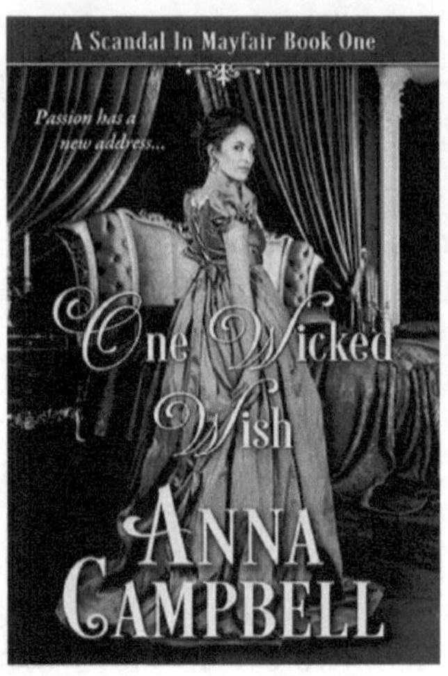

Her secret lover...

Stella Faulkner has been a despised poor relation in her odious uncle's house since she was forced to flee Italy ahead of Napoleon's invasion. In return for a roof over her head, she acts as her cousin's unpaid governess and companion. Stella knows that if she shows the slightest trace of her disgraced mother's wildness, she'll be cast out to face destitution. But after ten years of thankless servitude, Stella encounters a dashing libertine who turns her world to flame. Handsome Lord Halston is irresistible, but every kiss, every caress carries the risk of discovery, and with discovery, disaster.

The rake beguiled...

Grayson Maddox, Earl of Halston, glories in his reputation for charm, seduction, and ruthlessness. His mistresses know that the profligate lord offers them pleasure and luxury, but when he says goodbye, the affair is over. To Halston, love is a sentimental myth and fidelity a trap. One night at a glittering ball, he sees a beautiful woman trying to fade into the crowd of dowdy chaperones and every instinct clamors to make this mysterious lady his. But all bets are off when Stella Faulkner promises to become the lover he'll never forget.

Forbidden passion.

Halston and Stella start a sizzling affair under the cover of a respectable house party at his country estate. But once this interval of heady delight comes to an end, what will become of the humble governess and the wicked earl? Must they return to being strangers as they originally arranged, or will five days of intoxicating sin turn into forever?

Two Secret Sins: A Scandal in Mayfair Book 2

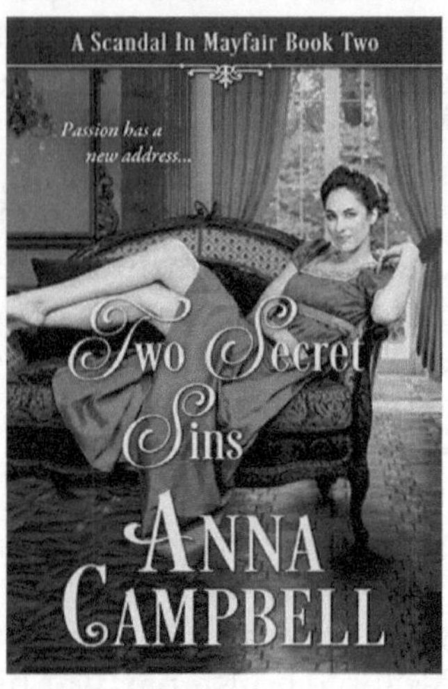

The Saint and the Sinner!

Eliot Ridley, Viscount Colville, is a man of immaculate character with lifelong ambitions to make his mark in parliament. Lady Verena Gerard is a headstrong, independent widow with a string of lovers in her scandalous past. Two people with absolutely nothing in common, apart from the irresistible desire that draws them into an explosive, secret affair.

Now Eliot is so determined to claim the reckless beauty as his own that he's ready to throw away his stainless reputation and his political hopes. What choice does Verena have when he proposes but to end the liaison? Taking a notorious woman as his wife will taint Eliot and his family, not to mention that after the brutal misery of her first marriage, she's vowed never to wed again.

Never say never.

In the glamorous, sophisticated world Eliot and Verena inhabit, wickedness thrives behind closed doors and the only unforgivable sin is falling in love. Will the handsome viscount defy society and Verena's fears to win the bride he wants? Or will Eliot and his wild lady part to follow their separate destinies and forever spurn the forbidden longing in their hearts?

Three Times Tempted:
A Scandal in Mayfair Book 3

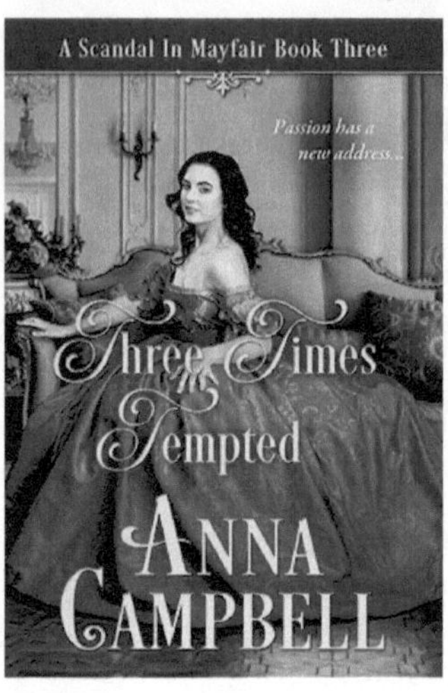

A secret rebel...

Beautiful, spirited Lady Imogen Ridley is the toast of London's glamorous season. Her blue-blooded admirers would be shocked to know that beneath her glittering veneer, she loathes society's shallow snobberies. All she wants is to return to her gardening projects in the country.

Her reckless attempt to spark a scandal that will result in a quick trip home goes awry when she meets a handsome stranger in a dark gazebo. A string of forbidden trysts follow that fateful encounter, as immediate attraction soon turns to blazing passion. But Imogen has been promised to another, and her father is powerful and ruthless. He won't tolerate any challenge to his ambitions for his daughter.

***A man from a different world...**

American Caleb Black finds himself at odds with England's hidebound rules. Despite his wealth and brilliance as a landscape designer, he's considered little better than a servant in status-obsessed Mayfair. So when he sets his sights on marrying the Earl of Deerforth's lovely daughter, he knows he's asking for trouble.

And trouble is exactly what he gets. Caleb needs to call on all his cleverness and determination to court his exquisite lady, let alone engineer a chance to make her his. With every secret meeting, every stolen caress, desire burns hotter, while danger and disgrace loom ever closer. Will this impossible love affair shatter the towering barriers of class and pedigree? Or will noble lineage, family duty, and centuries of tradition forever separate this man of the people from his aristocratic beloved?

Four Christmas Kisses:
A Scandal in Mayfair Book 4

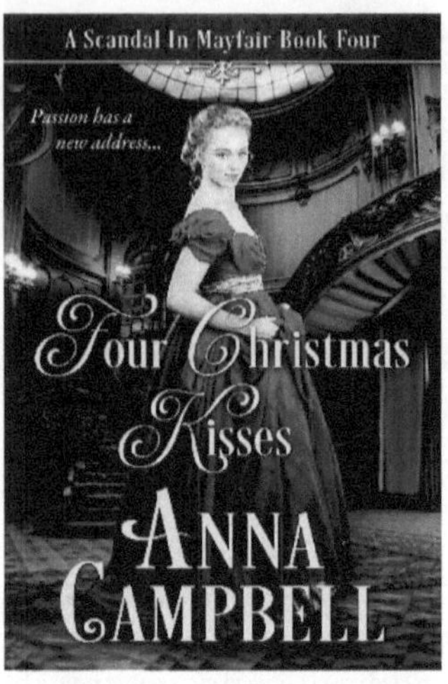

A mysterious guest at Christmas.

Spirited Anthea Bryars already has enough problems to deal with when a few days before Christmas, she stumbles across an unconscious stranger in the woods. She and her half-sisters will be homeless after New Year, now that Lord Denton has inherited Yardley Hall and given the family their marching orders. The last thing Anthea needs is a handsome, smart-mouthed distraction who makes her long for forbidden pleasures.

Secrets and passion...

After rakish Christopher Trant, Earl of Denton, tumbles from his horse in a snowstorm, his rescuer is the loveliest woman he's ever seen. But waking up the next morning, he's horrified to discover that at Yardley Hall, he's universally hated as Wicked

Cousin Christopher. He'd left London assuming the remote manor house was empty, but it turns out it's occupied by three unknown cousins and an alluring lady called Anthea. To play for time, he pretends that his injuries have stolen his memory. But one small lie leads to others, until he's so tangled in desire and deception, he doesn't know where to turn.

A season of goodwill?

Will the revelation of Christopher's identity destroy all his chances to win Anthea? Or might the magic of Christmas unite these two unlikely lovers and conjure up a bright new future for the whole family? Could four Christmas kisses mean goodbye or happy forever after.

www.ingramcontent.com/pod-product-compliance
Lightning Source LLC
Chambersburg PA
CBHW062001190726
48285CB00003BA/781